NEMO

INTO *the* ABYSS *and* BACK

MARK L. DERDZINSKI

Inspired by *20,000 Leagues Under the Sea* by Jules Verne

Artwork & Design by Joe Spix and Kristin Spix

ACKNOWLEDGEMENTS

This tale comprises many stories as part of its creation. It began when I was a child and my father would read to me the stories of Jules Verne. This was the story of how a writer ignited the imaginations of a father and son.

For years, I watched my mother work in watercolor, charcoal, and oil. I wanted desperately to create those landscapes as well. She encouraged me to always work hard at whatever medium I chose. This was the story of learning discipline and understanding perseverance.

For years, my wife and son both prompted me to tell the tale. My wife helped me to give depth to my characters, even the robotic ones. My son, on the other hand, made sure that the Nautlius was, above all things, really cool! He helped model the robots through countless Lego versions of DOC and Ulysses. This was the story of a family having fun and creating something together.

My nephew Joe and his wife Kristin patiently worked with me during the design of the cover art and the process of typesetting. Their artistry, professionalism, and generosity are truly marvelous. This was the story about enthusiasm and collaboration between creators.

Jeremy Shermak, my colleague and friend, helped me work through the process of finding the right tenor and choosing the right words. Editing doesn't come close to describing the insights he never failed to offer. This was a story of collegiality and creativity.

Each person is a part of this book, each a page in the story of its creation. Each has my deepest gratitude.

Contents

1

THE PASSENGER

Alicia Petit-Smith awoke with a start. Sitting upright in a bed, she then crumpled back into the pillow, her eyes watering as pain coursed through her head. She was slightly aware of movement in the room and she smelled faintly the salty sea air, yet it seemed distant and piped in rather than immediate. A green light pulsed through the film of her tears, and a masculine voice that was synthesized and without a human's warm tone, pronounced, rather than said, "Captain, the patient has awakened. Pulse is 110, BP: 140 over 90; oxygen –normal." There was no response. She reached to wipe her eyes when a tissue was placed into her hand. She took it, quickly dabbed her eyes, and stared at the figure leaning over her bed. Her head began to pound again, and her voice barely rasped, "Where…"

"You are safe aboard ship. I am the Captain. You are the only survivor of…," the voice paused, searching for the appropriate words, "a terrible incident."

At that moment she dreamed she saw a mechanical figure move toward her other side, reaching above her head. She had just become aware of the I.V. in her left arm, when the voice said soothingly, "You rest now." And then all was darkness.

A series of blurred dreams of suffocating water and high-pitched screams disturbed her sleep. She tried to scream, to awaken, but could never make it to the surface of that helpless lethargy that is the nightmare. A deep shuddering and screeching coursed throughout her central nervous system. The episode played itself out and began again in an endless loop. Finally, it was too much; she clawed at the dark space about her and tried to inhale the scorching air into her aching lungs and screamed.

She was awake. Her head hurt but not as badly as before. She saw clearly a small circle of green light flashing above a bulkhead door. She caught something in her periphery and instinctively turned toward it on her left side. She shrunk back in bed. A mechanical body and head began to move toward her while raising two black rubber, human-like arms and hands.

"Get back! Stay away from me you bastard!"

Desperately, she looked around for a weapon. Anatomically, the machine was designed to resemble a human's form. A broad torso sat upon spindly metal legs that resembled those of an ostrich. The disproportion would have been laughable if it weren't for the foreboding, faceless head with backlit eye sockets. Those eyes glowed a soft green hue and then suddenly changed to blue. From within the head a voice loudly sounded, "Please be still; I am a medic/combat unit assigned to medical detail. I am not a threat."

It moved toward Alicia; its arms reached forward with open hands in a gesture meant to calm.

"Touch me and you'll pay..."

"DOC, disengage!"

Instantly the machine stopped. "Retain medic mode."

"Aye, sir," the machine reported, and the previous soft green light emanated from the eye sockets.

"Lucky for you," Alicia shot back. "And if you don't keep your toy away from me, I'll bust its head, then yours! Just where the hell am I?"

"Some temper," the voice cut in, lingering over the syllables of her name, "Ms. Petit-Smith." She froze in place.

"How do you know who I am? Just who the hell are you, and where am I?"

"Come now, you always get your quarry Ms. Petit-Smith, and this time was no exception. Although, I believe you got more than you bargained for."

"No! It can't be...is it really you?"

"You may refer to me as Nemo."

Nemo approached her bedside, and she put her hands in a defensive posture born of formal training in the martial arts. Instantly, a whirring noise began and the machine on the other side of the bed flew into motion. Blades unfolded and several electrodes began sparking as the head disappeared into the torso. There was a blur of movement as the wide torso sprang onto the bed. Instantly Alicia felt herself pressed into the foam mattress with crushing weight. Her arms were being pulled over her head and would, with very little effort, be pulled off her body in a few moments. She couldn't breathe and as she tried to move her head, a carbon stiletto pushed ever so lightly against her forehead.

"Without any other weapons, DOC could take out a company of fully armed U.S. SEALS—in fact, he has. So if you want to try out your strip mall black belt, be my guest. It's your move, make it a good one. I'll be washing you out of the bilge after lunch." With that, Nemo left the room.

The strain on her arm sockets increased. She would cry out but could not breathe. Blood began to trickle from the small puncture in her forehead.

"O—kay" she coughed.

"Repeat!" blasted the machine above her.

"I won't try..." and she passed out.

Nemo had been just outside the opened door. "Full resuscitation!"

"Aye, sir!"

As quickly as it had transformed into an instrument of torture, the machine was working at saving human life. An extra pair of arms appeared and it simultaneously treated the wound on the patient's head, positioned the arms and applied bracing, and began to change the solution in the I.V. Nemo smiled at the efficiency with which his machinery worked.

2

Coming to Terms

After some period of time, Alicia awoke in the same bed as before. This time, though, there was no green light blinking over the door. She looked to her left for her nurse-jailer, but it was not present. The clothes she had been wearing at the time of the wreck were draped over a chair in the room. She looked down and saw that the I.V. had been removed. She noticed a note propped up on the stand next to her bed:

There is a steward outside your room. He'll bring you breakfast if you need to eat. If not, he'll escort you topside. –N

Alicia slowly swung her legs over the side of the bed and approached her clothes. "The bastard probably raped me when I was out," she huffed as she dressed. She remembered having interviewed victims of date rape who had been drugged. They almost always said that even though they could not remember what happened, they nonetheless knew they had been somehow violated. Alicia's intuition, though, gave her no such indication.

Outside the door she found the steward. Like his colleague, he was humanoid, made of metal and black rubber. He turned briskly and his eyes glowed orange.

"Breakfast, ma'am?"

The question at first caught her off guard, but only for a moment.

"Uh, no, take me to your boss, now!"

"Yes, ma'am. Follow me."

The machine moved briskly; its legs and feet minced like a dancer's. The passage-way seemed more like a corridor in an office building than a ship. It was at least ten feet wide and the ceiling was eight feet, even with all the exposed pipe work overhead. It was bright and seemed to be lit with natural light. The walls were white and every few feet there was what seemed like a large barcode painted on the wall. Suddenly, they stopped.

"Watch your step, ma'am."

The machine extended a hand to assist her up a flight of steep stairs.

"My legs aren't broken," she scolded, and ascended the stairs.

"Ma'am, mind the deck!"

As Alicia came to the top step, she slipped backward and the steward caught her before she fell. Her feet were dangling above the steel decking. The steward was holding her from under her arms. She grimaced in pain. Below her, two immense torrents of water rushed over a portion of the decking and then divided into large funnels that ended somewhere inside the ship. Tens of thousands of gallons were passing through by the minute. Despite this deluge of water, there was an eerie quietness about the deck. The only sound was the hull's crisp tearing through the ocean's surface and the constant moan of the wind. She had been blown backward by the rush of air passing over the superstructure. The commotion caught Nemo's attention.

"Steward, cradle her and bring her here," commanded Nemo

"Aye, sir."

The pain eased as the machine shifted its burden. Alicia noticed that the black rubber covering on the steward's arms and hands was as smooth as a child's skin. With perfect balance, the machine skipped from the stairs and over a short ladder to where Nemo was standing behind a protective wall of the ship's conning tower.

"Set her down; remain here."

The robot gently set Alicia's feet on the deck as it continued to support her back until she was standing on her own. Nemo nodded toward her and in a familiar manner asked, "So, how are you?"

Alicia smoldered with anger. She could not, however, act out. This was the most immediate threat to her life she ever faced.

"I see you left your bodyguard below."

"Have I?"

Alicia realized the emptiness of her statement. She looked out over the vast expanse of water around them. The ship was moving at a breathtaking speed. The horizon was nothing but ocean. Even falling off the deck would be deadly as the hull moved through the water with impossible speed. Without looking at her, Nemo spoke,

"I'll be sure to take you to the nearest port feasible. Your passage back to the United States shall be provided. If you insist upon resistance and retribution, you'll be treated accordingly. You have forced me to defend myself once and if you continue to do so, you shall pay the price. In the meantime, try to make yourself comfortable on board. The steward shall serve you accordingly."

"Shove it!"

"Very well. Steward, take Ms. Petit-Smith below decks; confine her to the empty locker on C deck, and see that she is escorted at all times to and from the head. If she tries to escape or proves violent, assume self-defense mode."

"Aye, sir!"

At that moment the very tip of Alicia's fourth and fifth knuckles caught Nemo's chin. Instinctively, his head turned away as the fist made contact. The force of the blow had been reduced by the quick reaction of the robot that had wrapped one arm under Alicia's armpit and slammed her body into itself. The long forearm extended across her chest and pinned her other arm to her side. Her body was perpendicular to the robot's chest and the pressure being exerted pinned her striking arm to the robot. The other black rubber hand spread over her face and, covering her mouth, nose, and eyes, began to press its rubber skinned, titanium fingers into her temples. She tried to stamp her heel into the robot's foot to break its bones. She succeeded, however, only to split open her heel and turn her ankle over. The grip on her head and the lack of air were taking effect and her body began to go limp.

"Uncover her face."

The black hand was withdrawn.

"Hey..." Nemo grasped her chin and shook her face, "Wake up; yes, wake up. You have a choice. Do you want to be crushed to death or drown in the ocean?"

The robot's grip increased.

"Well?"

"F-f-f-" —another jolt of force stopped her breath.

"I'm sorry, what was that?" Nemo leaned closer and cupped his hand to his ear in mockery.

"Home!" was the last word she exhaled before she lost consciousness.

"Home!" Nemo said to himself and considered her response for a few moments. "Let her down slowly and carefully."

The robot released its grip and the seemingly lifeless body slid to the deck.

"She's got guts; I'll give her that. Though, I shouldn't be surprised."

The robot stood without responding. It never responded, of course, but Nemo still occasionally made one-sided conversations with it from time to time, especially when he was uncertain as to what to do next. He gazed out over the horizon for several minutes. Without averting his eyes, he ordered, "Take her to sick bay." Nemo held his watch to his mouth and pushed a button at the two o'clock position.

"DOC, report to sick bay; perform diagnostic scans and, if stable, proceed to treating wounds."

"Aye, sir."

Nemo turned to the robot at his side, "Secure for dive."

"Aye, sir, secure for dive."

The robot had no sooner said this when a buzzer sounded throughout the ship, audible on deck. A previously unseen hatch opened at his feet and Nemo made his way down the steeply inclined steps. The decks were already awash as the hatch hissed close above his head.

On his way to sick bay, Nemo turned right into a small alcove with panels of colored lights and various displays with images and numbers constantly moving across the screens. He depressed a button and issued the command: "Make depth 40 meters, slow to 5 knots, maintain bearing. Sweep for any unidentified vessels. Signal alarm at first contact."

He walked briskly but unhurriedly through the main level corridor. It was a long ship and he walked a full half minute before he came within proximity to the entrance. The smell of antiseptic and the plastic aroma of newly opened first aid kits permeated the air. He turned in and walked directly up to the bed. She was awake, alert, and watching the robot treat her cut heel. Without looking at him she hissed, "You're lucky you have protection."

"You're lucky I have patience," he returned.

Her head shot up and she locked eyes with Nemo; the hatred burned deeply.

"As I said before, as soon as I can take you to a safe port, I will. In the meantime, try to relax and be civil. You'll be treated accordingly and enjoy some freedoms aboard."

"Freedom!?!" she interrupted. "Freedom within my own prison cell is more like it!"

Alicia bolted upright in bed and unexpectedly collided with the heel of Nemo's right hand to her sternum. The pain cut through her upper body and she tried to catch her breath as her head hit the pillow.

"If you succeed in killing me, Ms. Petit-Smith, this submarine will most certainly become your prison cell and eventual tomb. None of my crew would ever obey you. Any attempt to control the vessel would trigger them to restrain you, much as you were restrained on deck. You're on board and there are only two ways out. You can cooperate and, when feasible, be delivered to a safe port from which you'll make your way back to the U.S. All necessary means will be at your disposal. The other route is for your remains to be jettisoned. My safety is your ticket off this vessel. Don't mistake it."

Alicia stared at him and he looked deeply into her smoky hazel eyes. Violence quivered there and then, like a candle's flame, snuffed out. The realization took hold and she knew that he understood this. Nemo changed the topic:

"Are you hungry?"

"Yes, I am. I could use something to drink, too."

Nemo looked toward the robot and, in an eerie, human manner, the robot confirmed her statement, "The patient is mildly dehydrated and glucose levels are low." Nemo held his watch to his mouth, "Steward, luncheon will be served in the forward salon."

"Aye, sir" came the transmitted reply from someplace forward.

"Follow me, Ms. Petit-Smith."

Alicia hopped off the bed and, limping at first, made her way after Nemo. He strode quickly and she struggled to keep up for about twenty-five meters.

"How long is this boat?" Alicia whined, " I'm tired and I'm hungry!"

Nemo stopped outside an open bulkhead door. "Please join me Ms. Petit-Smith or if you prefer, you can take your lunch in your room." Nemo motioned for her to pass him and enter the room first.

Her mouth dropped. Before her was a vast space with tables and comfortable wing chairs, a chaise lounge, and in the center was an enormous oyster, as big around as a truck's wheel. In the middle of its ponderous halves was a fountain murmuring in soft cascades. The walls were bookshelves with what had to be thousands of volumes bound in different color leathers. The lights were bright, yet soft.

"Lunch is served," Nemo smiled slightly.

Just beyond the fountain and the main study area was a table some eight feet in length with a large chair on each end. The table heaped with food enough for a dozen hungry men. Alicia's hunger sharpened. She was about to rush at it but then paused.

"Please Ms. Petit-Smith, be seated. The steward shall serve you."

A better butler could not have been imagined. After seating her and placing the napkin in her lap, the robot began to offer her dishes while Nemo explained what they were.

"Everything in my galley is provided by the sea. I have nothing from the land."

Alicia took a cutlet from a plate held before her by the steward and cut a piece and began to eat.

"Except this. I know veal as well as anyone."

"Indeed, your uncle raised veal in Oklahoma, if I'm not mistaken."

She stopped chewing and looked crossly at Nemo who continued talking.

"This, though, isn't veal, Ms. Petit-Smith; it is fillet of sea turtle."

"Really," she deadpanned.

The cat and mouse game was irritating her, but not nearly as much as her hunger; she reached for a scone from a platter in front of her. As she was spreading marmalade, Nemo read her thoughts, "And that's not passion fruit or papaya, but sea cucumber."

She bit into the scone and, in spite of herself, smiled.

"It's good," she admitted.

Despite the vast number of dishes before her, Alicia managed to try a little of everything.

"Well, Nemo. The lunch was quite good. I must admit, this room is most impressive. I'd like to take a closer look at..."

Just then, the lights went out. Everything was dark, save for the glowing orange light of the steward's eyes. Suddenly the room was filled with a swirling blue light. The ceiling panels and a good portion of the walls had been slid back to reveal the sea around them. She was in the middle of a tremendous observatory some forty meters below the surface of the sea!

"My God!" she exclaimed.

Attracted by the submarine's light, fish began to gather at the windows looking at the woman inside who, with mouth agape, gawked back at them in very much the same manner. Suddenly, the fish scattered and an immense shape materialized from out of the darker blue of the ocean. She involuntarily stepped back from the canopy as a large shark passed overhead, the maws bristling with rows of serrated teeth. Fascinated by his movement, she continued to walk back until she bumped into Nemo, himself.

"Mesmerizing, isn't it?"

Suddenly she came to her senses and stepped two paces from Nemo.

"This is my world, my dominion, Ms. Petit-Smith. It is all I have, and all I shall ever need. The solitude, and the power that comes of that solitude— like that shark or that ray."

Nemo pointed toward a manta ray flying beside the observatory; its wingspan was at least twenty feet. Alicia started at the apparition just on the other side of the glass. As she began to study its lines and markings, it veered off and disappeared into the blinding blue. She felt her head growing heavy and her feet becoming light. She was caught just before her head would have struck the flooring.

3
THE DUEL

She was trying to breathe again and water was falling onto her head, into her mouth. Her lungs seared with the effort to take in the air, she clawed at the space above her and tried to scream, but was drowning in the blur of light and sound. Alicia bolted upright in bed. She was sweating profusely. She anxiously looked around, fearful of her surroundings. She was not in the room she originally had found herself. The bed she was in was large, king-sized. The linens were crisp and the blanket clutched in her hands was the softest she had ever felt. Alicia noticed that she was still dressed. Comforted by this, she began to take in the details of her new quarters. The room was large and well-furnished. A couple wardrobes were on one wall, while a dressing table and full-length mirror stood in one well-lit corner. A sink, toilet, and shower stall were discreetly positioned behind a partition that featured a mosaic of some sort of a golden shellfish in a field of lapis.

Thirsty, Alicia walked over to a small table where a decanter of crystal clear water sat. She filled a glass, replaced the decanter, took a hard swallow, and then gasped at what she saw. The decanter was slowly filling itself. There was no visible plumbing under the table top or faucet behind the table. "Who is this guy?" she wondered aloud. She walked over to the wardrobe and opened it. It had clothes in it, not unlike what Nemo wore, but fit for a woman's figure. There were hangers with pants draped over them and blouses with the same golden shellfish as the mosaic on the partition in the shower area. Her own clothes, admittedly, were in a sad state. There were smudges of grease that could not be washed out and there were tears in her jeans. Her shoes were a complete loss. The soles were pulling away from the uppers.

"Why not?" she concluded, and she took a pair of pants and a blouse from the wardrobe and a pair of slipper-like boots and walked over to the dressing table.

As she took her clothes off, she noticed her bruises and the many cuts and scrapes she sustained. She was aware that her lower back had been very sore since she first regained consciousness, but what she saw in the full-length mirror brought tears to her eyes. A livid, purple welt spanned her lower back and spread up toward the base of her ribcage. There were two distinct ruts that ran parallel about six inches apart. Something had obviously pinned her at some time.

Once dressed, she stepped outside her room into the corridor. The steward was standing at attention about ten feet away.

"Do you need anything, ma'am?"

"No, where's Nemo?"

"The Captain is in the forward study; I'll take you there presently."

Alicia followed the robot down the same path she had walked before. Eerily, the robot motioned for her to enter much the same way Nemo had.

Nemo was seated on one of the plush chairs, his feet upon an ottoman. He puffed a cigar while turning the pages of a considerable dossier. He arose as she entered.

"Ah. Ms. Petit-Smith. Do you mind?" and he gestured toward the robusto in his right hand.

"What? No. Go ahead. If I had a cigarette, I'd join you."

"Help yourself," offered Nemo, and he gestured toward an elegant silver tray on a nearby table that displayed a collection of cigars, cigarettes, and loaded pipes.

"And smoke in good health, Ms. Petit-Smith. These tobacco products are not only enjoyable, but entirely free of any carcinogens. There are no cancer-causing chemicals to be found."

"Don't tell me you're in league with Philip-Morris?"

"Ms. Petit-Smith," Nemo scolded, "I have nothing to do with the land. I harvest a certain seaweed from the Sargasso Sea. Philip-Morris is stuck in the same old rut of an exhausted cash crop."

As Alicia lit a cigarette, Nemo continued, "Still, I can understand your reference to Big Tobacco. It says here," Nemo reached for the thick folder he had been leafing through, "that you not only helped blow the whistle on Big Tobacco's fraud, but you personally attacked the architects of the monopoly, exposing domestic abuse, substance abuse, even obtaining undercover photos. That's impressive, considering the safety risks involved. But then again, you were always about taking risks."

Alicia coldly stared at him from behind a vale of smoke; tensely, she goaded him, "go on."

"When you were sixteen, you hid in the back of the high school principal's Suburban and recorded the lewd sounds of a sexual encounter between the principal and a student. You leveraged that information to get him to help with your placement in a top journalism program that your cash-strapped parents could not afford because of your mother's gambling debts. Once safely in the program, you exposed him two years later. This only propelled your career."

"And if I hadn't, he would still be abusing students."

"Why the two-year wait?"

"Why do you sink ships, kill people, and devastate families?"

"My campaign is self-defense. Which brings me to your latest effort."

"Hey, bullshit! You sunk a freighter with some five-hundred refugees aboard—women and children! Are you going to tell me that they attacked you!?!"

"They were combatants."

"You're a sick bastard."

"That vessel contained no fewer than fifty Al-Qaeda operatives."

"Yeah, right. You could say anything."

Nemo walked over to a desk, opened a drawer and pulled out a thick leather portfolio, and walked back to where Alicia stood, placing it into her hands. "This is all the information. I cross-referenced all the names on the ship's manifest with all the Al-Qaeda aliases. But you can read this at your leisure." She looked confused as she ran her fingers back through her hair.

"So you work for the U.S. military?"

"No."

"The CIA?"

"No."

"Well, damn it, who!?!"

"I work for no government, but for myself—same as you."

Nemo regained his chair and Alicia sat in an identical chair opposite him.

"I'm an award winning journalist for the Washington Post and I have an immensely successful, influential blog."

"The Post pays you, sure, but you had to finance much of your last assignment yourself. No one wanted to underwrite research that could end up with loss of life and most certainly a sunken vessel. Most people thought the sinkings were the work of U.S. Special Forces. How did you figure out that it wasn't?"

Alicia paused and thought of keeping silent but reconsidered and rejoined the duel that Nemo had begun. "It wasn't that difficult, really. Sinkings were occurring simultaneously in parts of the world where the U.S. couldn't possibly be, even given the vast resources of the military. Memos were flying between various departments in the Pentagon, trying to figure out who was coordinating all the carnage. Eventually, everyone was on the same page; that is, everyone knew what operations the U.S. had going and when and where. No other country had quite the resources or tactical wherewithal to do this without detection.

Then some alarming messages were coming through the Pacific Fleet Headquarters. U.S. hunter subs were pursuing sonar blips that weren't quite like anything in their files. It wasn't quite a mammal and it wasn't quite metal. The fact that a Virginia-class sub was unable to pursue it for lack of speed and diving capability signaled some sort of new submarine. Since Intelligence confirmed that no one else could possess a sub of such advanced design, especially without any records of outsourcing components from the usual suspects, I figured it had to be some maniacal rogue. I was right."

"Bravo, Ms. Petit-Smith, bravo! I underestimated your resourcefulness. How, though, did you know that shallow water is the Nautilus' Achilles heel?"

Alicia lightly touched the insignia on her blouse as she heard the ships' name, remembering the shellfish mosaic in her room. She paused, looked up at Nemo, but it had been enough; he called her bluff: "You didn't know! It was coincidence that your conventional sonar tracked me. Of course! Shallow, warm water like that in the Persian Gulf is tough for any submarine to hide in. Once initial contact is made, the game is up!"

"I'm hungry," Alicia said.

"But of course," Nemo replied, "steward, prepare the dining room for Ms. Petit-Smith's lunch."

"You're not eating?"

"Who can eat with so much work to do!?!"

Nemo stood up, bowed slightly in her direction and, crushing out his cigar in a shell ashtray, left.

Alicia sat reflecting upon the conversation she just had, if one could call it a conversation. It was more of a debriefing. He is testing the waters, she concluded, learning about what the world knows of him through her, the best investigative reporter around. She would have done the same if the roles were reversed. Still, he is unstable, unpredictable. At one moment he is having her executed, the next he is offering a gourmet lunch.

She began eating another shrimp cocktail when the soup was served.

"What's this?"

"Conch chowder, ma'am."

Alicia pushed the bits of conch around the bowl.

"Something wrong, ma'am?"

"No, "Alicia replied, "I just don't have much of an appetite after all. I'd just like some coffee."

"Certainly."

The steward returned from a nearby sideboard with a steaming cup and a creamer and sugar bowl.

"Where are we? Longitude and latitude, I mean."

"I'm sorry, ma'am; I cannot provide that information. Perhaps you should ask the Captain."

"Yeah, right."

"Shall, I call the Captain for you?"

"No, never mind. He's no more helpful than you are."

The robot stared, the orbs of soft orange steady and unwavering. Alicia thought for a moment, then added, "Actually there is one thing. Is there any way I could take a bath?"

"Yes, ma'am. There is a shower in your state room and the Nautilus does have a Turkish bath."

"A Turkish bath?"

"Yes, ma'am. Please follow me."

Alicia pushed away from the table and followed the robot through a door at the far end of the long dining hall.

4

ENGINEER AND ARTIST

Through the doorway, the robot led her down two flights of twenty stairs and turned down a corridor lined with mahogany paneling. Pausing, the robot pushed gently against a brass door pull and motioned for Alicia to enter. Inside, Alicia found a legitimate Turkish bath. The walls were covered in mosaics of underwater seascapes. Several small pools seemed to overlap one another. One was a whirlpool; one was a mineral bath, while one was for actual bathing; one for rinsing; and another was larger, for swimming or just lounging. Towels were kept on heated bars and there was a massage table off to one side.

"A toilet is accessed through the door at the back of the bath," the steward explained, pointing toward the back of the room.

"Well! Your boss might be certifiable, but he knows the better things. I don't suppose he gives massages," Alicia added nodding toward the massage table.

"I am qualified in therapeutic as well as Swedish massage and acupuncture. I am authorized to provide massage therapy."

Alicia involuntarily stepped back. "Uh, thank you, but no."

"Will you be bathing?"

"I haven't brought any clothes with me."

"All shall be provided. Enjoy your time."

With that, the steward left the bath and stationed himself outside the door.

Looking sheepishly around, Alicia paused, then undressed, leaving her clothes where they fell. She descended the tiled steps into the bubbling mineral pool and eased in upon the seat. She looked upward and gasped in surprise. Above the entire bath house, the domed ceiling was occupied by an extravagant mosaic of a tremendous octopus whose arms radiated from the center and descended down around the walls, gripping the room. The arms of the grand creature shimmered in various hues of golden olive, tinged with crimson accents. The suckers were actually the halves of oysters affixed to the tiles, each one offering a large, milky pearl. The background was a mix of every hue of ocean blues and violets. It seemed as though the lapis eyes looked back at her, yet there was something palpably calming about this colossus, and she smiled and nodded in response to this inquisitive work of imagination reaching from above her.

The mineral salts worked wonders for her sore back. She was about to leave the pool to walk around to enter the bathing pool when she noticed that the two pools intersected, yet there was no door or gate that had to be opened. She waded to the intersection and noticed that the waters retained their respective currents and colors, yet she could pass from one to the other. She emitted a slight laugh. "That is so cool! How did he..." And she suddenly caught herself. She resisted combining her admiration for the technology with the engineer.

The bathing pool was suffused with a soap and moisturizing solution the likes of which she never encountered. Her skin felt smooth and, odd to say, relaxed. From the bathing pool she passed into the rinsing pool which was cold at first. She could feel the residue of the bathing pool being washed off in the circular current. As she moved toward the stairs leading out of the pool, the water temperature gradually warmed to match her own body temperature. As she ascended the stairs, the railing presented a heated shelf with a towel, the softest she had ever felt. As she patted herself dry, she sensed that something was different. She looked at her arms and legs; the cuts and scrapes had lost their painful redness, and the skin was nearly smooth. Her injuries were barely perceptible!

"My God, what have I found!" she exclaimed. "I can't take this tight-lipped nonsense anymore. This guy may be nuts, he may be evil, but what he can do! Steward!"

The robot entered the room carrying a fresh change of clothes, "Ma'am?"

"Take me to Nemo!"

"I cannot, ma'am."

"What?!? Oh, right. I'll get dressed first."

"I cannot. The Captain has commanded not to be disturbed."

"You have got to be joking!"

The robot stared at her.

"Of course not, you don't joke. Well, what are my options?"

"You may visit the forward salon, the dining room, the gallery, the museum of the natural world, the main library, and, of course, your stateroom." Alicia dropped the towel she had been holding around her.

"You require assistance," the robot responded, and began to move toward her.

"Don't touch me! Just leave the towel. I'll dress and meet you in the hall."

"Yes, ma'am."

As soon as the door closed after the robot, Alicia turned and rushed toward the toilet where she threw up the little bit of lunch she had consumed. After flushing the toilet, she sat atop the commode and held her head in her hands which felt like someone else's hands on the skin of her face. Just yesterday she was being crushed to death by a robot at the order of a modern pirate. The same pirate then put her up in a spacious stateroom complete with gourmet food and a full-time valet. There was even a spa and all the amenities of a posh resort, but even better: refilling decanters and miraculous healing baths. It was a bit much to comprehend, even for Alicia. Still wary, but absolutely convinced of her need to acquiesce given the circumstances, all she could do was to dress and take in the other attractions aboard.

The gallery's hall was at least fifty long strides in length, with a center aisle that contained cases of jewelry. There were several Van Goghs considered to have been lost and a couple that were outright stolen. There was a sketchbook of Da Vinci's technical drawings, the only copy of it in existence. Every major period of Western European Art was represented. Both paintings and sculpture adorned the brightly lit space.

As she made her way toward the end of the hall, the steward met her.

"Ma'am, two hours have elapsed. Would you care for refreshment?"

Alicia had completely lost track of the passage of time; it seemed like only some few minutes had passed.

"Yes, I would."

"Tea shall be served in the forward salon."

The robot escorted Alicia through a series of corridors that bypassed the gallery and she found herself being conducted into the forward salon once again. An immense silver trolley of teas and cookies and finger sandwiches was wheeled toward where she sat at the table. Her mouth opened in delight.

"May I serve?"

"Of course," and in spite of herself, Alicia said "please."

She sat alone and ate. Only the sound of her own chewing and her sipping of tea was audible. The steward stood some twelve feet away, the electronic orbs glowing orange, all silence, without breath. It certainly wasn't the executioner called DOC. It was, nonetheless, an able, efficient killer. When it carried her to the bridge on deck, though, its rubber-like arms were soft and even tender in a way; there was the slight resistance and yielding of human flesh. The same as the first robot—ah, but what terrible potential! Nemo had saved her life even as he was in the process of killing. Why? Why would anyone do this? She took another sandwich. He was insane, monstrous, evil. She was his prisoner, watched by his robotic jailers. It was only a matter of time before this maniacal fiend would rape her and kill her. Alicia sipped her tea and nervously took a bite.

She remembered, though, that she had not been raped when there had been an opportunity for Nemo to do so. Perhaps he was waiting for the "right moment", whatever that meant to his sick mind. She was, after all, watched at all times. Yet, if she didn't have the run of the ship, she had relatively free access and movement. She thought of the half-consumed sandwich in her hand. Scallops with a seaweed and what seemed to be a garlic spread. At least her last meal would be a good one.

Alicia's reverie was broken by a shrill horn blasting throughout the ship. A mechanical voice sounded throughout, "Prepare battle stations!" Alicia had spilled her tea and the steward was handing her a napkin saying, "To your stateroom, to your stateroom!" The robot began to shoo her out of the salon.

"What's happening!?! Are we being attacked!?!"

"I cannot say. Please proceed to your stateroom."

Alicia stalled, asking questions, "Where is Nemo? Are we safe? Can I take cigarettes with me?" Just then DOC appeared, the head sucked down into the torso and an extra set of ugly, bare, steel arms perched on its back in right angles, like diabolic wings.

"All subjects must be secured. Take to assigned quarters, lock-down, and issue sedative if necessary. Execute."

"Aye, sir!" the steward shot back.

Without pause, it scooped Alicia into the crook of one arm and bounded down the corridor.

"Put me down! Hey, you ...! Put me down!"

Once outside her stateroom, the door opened automatically and the robot paused, took a calculation and then tossed Alicia through the air some twenty feet and into her bed, landing her back first.

"You son of a ..." but the door closed on her voice and sealed with a hiss.

Though her bruises, especially her back, were sore from the landing, she wasn't injured. The room began to tilt toward the bow, at first only slightly but then increasing to about fifteen degrees. Nothing, however, moved in the room. All the furnishings were secured to the decking and the walls. The water in the basins and toilet had been drained. Alicia began to feel a little woozy; the pressure in her ears increased and her neck and head felt hot. The room tilted another five degrees. It was the first time since being topside that she felt forward movement and increasing velocity. Suddenly a deep, instant shudder sounded through her room. Alicia felt it deep within her bowels. A moment later another, closer, shock caused her intestines to seize and then drop within her body. Stricken and ill, she felt herself slide across the linens of her bed toward the pitched floor. Disoriented, she lay crumpled on the floor and closed her eyes.

5

UNDER ATTACK

Semi-conscious, she saw the orange glow of the steward's eyes and then noticed the soft blue glow of those of DOC.

"Shall I take her to medical, Captain?"

"No, she'll be more comfortable here. Prepare a syringe of an antacid."

"Aye, sir."

Alicia lay there not moving. Nemo knelt by her side and offered his hand to help her up. Her eyelids closed and tears pressed from beneath them. Nemo paused and became aware of DOC's presence.

"The injection is prepared, Captain."

"You need a shot to stabilize your stomach," Nemo spoke to the bent person on the floor, "just stay on your side and DOC will administer it in the buttock."

Alicia said nothing as Nemo pulled back the waistband of her pants. DOC gently pulled up some skin and expertly administered the medication.

"There, not so bad," smiled Nemo. Alicia did not reply.

"Captain, shall I place the patient in bed?" Before Nemo could answer, Alicia spoke, "No! I'll do it myself! I'm not crippled and I'm not a child!"

Alicia reached up to the side of the mattress and began to pull herself up when her equilibrium began to fail. Nemo caught her in his arms before she fell backward. He then put one arm under her back and swept his other arm under her legs and stood up straight. He stepped toward the bed and was laying her down when he noticed that her eyes were staring through their tears and were taking in the features of his face. Though distracted by her nausea, she still examined his face and looked into his eyes, gauging, learning. Uncomfortable, he turned his head away as he set her down.

"Now. If you'll excuse me..."

"What happened?" Alicia asked.

"I need to attend to some things," Nemo replied and was walking toward the door.

"We were attacked, weren't we? It was the Navy, wasn't it?" Alicia's voice began to rise, "They're looking for us, aren't they? Hunting us? They don't even know I'm down here. They'll kill us!"

Anger began to replace the fear and even the sickness that she had been feeling. Nemo stopped short and spun on his heel.

"Yes. Yes, the United States Navy is hunting us. And if you think knowledge of your presence aboard would somehow alter their course of action then you are, indeed, a child. Right now they are blanketing the surface with sonar buoys to ascertain whether their two torpedoes had, in fact, struck our hull.

We are by no means safe. Before a naval task force with submarine escort can get here, we'll need to leave the area. If you please, I have work to do."

With that, Nemo strode out.

6

THE WEATHER-GAUGE

Standing within the conn, which was the central control center for the submarine's operations and maneuvers, Nemo squinted at the large liquid crystal display. A graphic bar filled up with blue light and registered the message: 100% reception/transmissions/50 mile. Nemo reached across to a large digital timer on the wall and pushed a button, commencing a countdown. Three minutes is all he needed and then he would know what his options were. A message light began blinking on the panel. Nemo moved a computer mouse on a pad and selected a prompt that read, text message. The ship was observing total silence. An email appeared on the screen:

Patient requests to leave room and to talk with you.

Nemo responded:

Negative. Keep patient in stateroom. Steward to stand guard in room. Seal door. If patient becomes loud, subdue without injury.

Affirmative, appeared in response.

Nemo looked up just as the timer reached the three minute mark. He then moved his curser on the screen to the prompt, retrieve, and then moved it over an option reading retrieval speed. Nemo entered the slowest setting possible. He then moved the cursor to an icon that resembled a screen and clicked. Instantly, several screens lit up and then their pictures were separated by various crawls and overlapping images with text appearing on all of them. This was all the information being broadcast in a 50 mile radius of the Nautilus' position. The Navy was trying to crowd as many assets as possible into the area. There was no word as to any submarine traffic which meant that either there wasn't any or that one was already on the scene in the immediate vicinity. Sonar buoys were pinging away at various depths and frequencies. Nemo moved toward the last screen which showed atmospheric conditions. He clenched his right fist in hopeful excitement.

Typhoon season was reaching its height and, fortunately for the Nautilus, it was doing its worst right now at the surface. Winds were blowing at near hurricane force and seas were very heavy. These conditions, combined with the number of sonar buoys in the area, would produce a cacophony of sound that would frustrate the search.

Surface ships would be seriously hindered in their movement. The only real threat was from other submarines. A reduction of threats was a priority, even if it meant risking detection by an attack submarine. It was a local threat, but without the added complications of surface and air assets. As fast as the Nautilus was, it was no match for airborne sub hunters. A message appeared on the display that the multi-link antenna had been retrieved and secured. Nemo typed a message to all crew:

Maintain silence. Rig for depth charge. Stealth operation. Text message only.

As soon as it was sent, minor systems began to shut down and the Nautilus began to operate on battery power only. Nemo proceeded down the stairs to the cockpit where he would actually drive the Nautilus himself. The space was large, with redundant systems to those in the conn, but with a rather large gimbal in the middle which contained a seat for a pilot. Nemo deftly climbed over the gimbal's superstructure and positioned himself in the seat. He placed a helmet on his head that featured a heads-up display on the inside of the visor that he lowered. On the display was a cursor that followed the movement of his right eye. As the cursor stopped at a given prompt, Nemo could activate that feature by blinking only his left eye once.

Nemo gripped two handles extending up from his chair, and the display, reading his fingerprints, lit up. Nemo did not care to use the photo-sensing prompts and instead, spoke softly into a microphone that extended from the side of the helmet below his chin.

"Make depth three meters from the bottom. Trace contour of seabed. Forward 10 knots."

The Nautilus instantly responded. Only the most essential mechanical elements were operating to accomplish the maneuvers. The display on the visor showed the Nautilus' progress within the area based upon known navigation charts. This mountainous area, though, with its many boulder fields, was hazardous without sweeping sonar readings. Even so, Nemo didn't want to risk operating that system, at least not yet. He steered the Nautilus in what appeared to be a middle road between close, overhanging structures on each side.

As treacherous as this was for the Nautilus, it was at least as dangerous for a following submarine. Once about ten miles from where the search was being conducted, he could activate the highly advanced forward sweeping sonar and literally drive the Nautilus through a maze of canyons. For now, though, it was a waiting game, and Nemo felt the sweat drip down his face.

After a little more than an hour, the log displayed in his visor showed that some twenty thousand yards had been covered. Nemo whispered into his microphone, "Activate forward sweep, nano-oscillation. Display forward view, 3-D." After about a second, an image appeared, filling Nemo's visor like the view out the windshield of a car. Though plants could not be seen, all geographical formations and features showed clearly. A corner of the display showed a map of the area some five thousand yards ahead of the Nautilus for 180 degrees. Nemo saw a large depression over a ridge to the port side and pulling back on the left handle, aimed the Nautilus for it. As the Nautilus passed over the ridge, the depth read 3000 feet along the bottom for at least five thousand yards. Nemo pulled back on the handles and whispered, "Maintain depth. All stop." The Nautilus glided over the deep area.

"Activate nano-oscillation. Three-six-zero degrees, 3-D."

This most comprehensive input would take a couple seconds to process. As the images came up on the screen, Nemo squinted to find something amiss either behind or below. "Infrared view," he commanded. A second later the screens showed various patches and hues of dark blues and violet. A smile spread over his face as sweat dripped down onto his tunic. Nemo gripped the handles. He whispered, "Open intakes, 100% volume, mark speed at control."

As he slid the handles forward and pushed down, the Nautilus nosed over into a forty-five degree attitude and the sea began flowing through the opened venturis. Like a rollercoaster passing the apex of a hill, the Nautilus shot down into the abyss. Nemo could feel his stomach compress and he smiled at the acceleration. The Nautilus was touching 100 knots when he began pulling back on the control handles. Heavy hydraulic pumps could be heard as the large propulsion nozzle, which served as both the means of propelling the vessel through the water as well as steering it, strained under the immense pressure being exerted by the surrounding sea. As smoothly as a roller coaster, the Nautilus leveled off and Nemo directed her flight some fifty feet from the bottom. He pushed the handles forward ever so slightly until the speed registered just over 110 knots.

The Nautilus sliced through the depths at that rate for more than two hours. Only at that time did Nemo begin to relax and slouch as little as he could in the snugly bolstered seat. They were now over the Equator and headed for an area that served absolutely no tactical advantage for any country possessing ballistic missile submarines. Nemo felt comfortable in turning over the driving to the automated system.

"Maintain contour of seabed at fifty feet. Ten knots, routine run. Sound all unidentified vessels at first contact, maintain 360 degree scan, level three."

With that, Nemo took off his helmet, placed it on its holder, climbed out of the gimbal and headed toward the Turkish bath.

As he patted himself dry an hour later, he noticed the silent alarm blinking on his watch that was setting atop his clothes. He reached over and spoke into it, "Yes? Cancel silent running."

The steward's voice sounded, "The passenger wishes to see you."

"Yes, of course. Show her to the forward salon; I'll be there presently. What meal is it?"

"Affirmative, sir. It is time for breakfast."

"Right. Put out a complete breakfast. Be sure to open the panels."

"Aye, sir."

Nemo thought as he dressed. She would have to be taken back and soon. But when? This latest attack necessitated some time away from populated waters and the usual search zones. The hidden port was the best place to be. It was, however, a solid seventy-two hours away from the present location and once inside, it would be too easy to find by the description she would give the Navy upon her return. The port contained all the heavy equipment and facilities needed to modify and when necessary, repair Nautilus.

Something else was troubling about the situation, something Nemo suspected but did not want to acknowledge. He felt as though the tables were somehow being turned on him and that he was somehow losing his advantage over his passenger. The worst of it was that he was letting this happen. He could not, however, say exactly why he felt this way.

7

The Seduction

As Nemo entered the salon he saw Alicia sitting at the breakfast table drinking coffee. She was wearing one of the bathrobes from the wardrobe in her room. Nemo involuntarily slowed his gait as he noticed the front of the robe opened to a rather revealing décolletage.

"Well, Nemo, I take it we won this round of playing pirates."

He ignored the comment as he extended his hand to receive the cup of hot coffee being placed in it by the steward.

"You know, I thought I was going to die. But then, deep down, I just knew that you'd find the way through it. It's a rather ironic position to be in. I hate your guts for what you have done to me and for keeping me prisoner, yet," and she paused taking a bite of sea cucumber and catching the juice as it ran down the corner of her mouth, "and yet, I'm actually rooting for you and your machinery."

As she finished, she crossed one leg over the other and the hem of the robe pulled over to the side to reveal her leg nearly to the hip.

"The great Captain Nemo, speechless?" she smiled.

And he was. It had been so long since he had been intimate, so long since he could be affected by even the shape of a woman's form. He felt his head beginning to swim. As he gazed down upon her, she shifted in her chair; the robe parted even more to reveal the open outline of her right breast cupped by the thick fold of material. He felt himself leaning toward her, like the slow motion fall between waking and dreaming. He stopped and stood upright. Something in his periphery caught his attention, and catching his breath, he turned quickly.

A white tip shark, attracted by the activity in the salon, was cruising about five meters from the glass. It wasn't large, white tips aren't, but its movements were so deliberate, so quick, and as he knew from experience, so terrible in their effect. Though it doesn't enjoy the same notoriety as the Great White, it was, perhaps, the most devastating of all sharks. Nemo's other instincts took precedence; he took a deep, full breath.

"You are very seductive Ms. Petit-Smith."

"Am I? I'll bet it's been a long time for you and…"

Nemo interrupted her, "And you know just what to do about it. Yes, yes. It's all about sex, I know. You would probably let me do what I would and then stick a knife in my back or do something more degrading."

She was sizing him up; contempt smoldered behind her eyes and she could feel the color rise up her neck. She untied the loosened sash of her robe and tucked one half of the robe over the other and then retied the sash securely. Nothing of her could be seen from the neck to her bare feet. Nemo took a sip of coffee.

"Your brother died a terrible death, did he not?"

"What the hell do you know about my brother!" she sprang from her chair.

"He overdosed on heroin, right?"

"Fuck you!"Alicia roared.

"Now, your brother obtained the heroin in Miami, where he was found dead."

Alicia stood staring at Nemo, shaking her head in disbelief.

"The Oliverez-Rancino cartel runs all the heroin into Miami these days. This cartel packs the drugs in the fuel tanks of commercial fishing vessels. The diesel fumes along with the pungent fish odor make it impossible for even the best canine units to detect. Very clever."

He paused and took a long drink from his cup.

"The reason that the U.S. Coastguard can't catch these people is because they keep looking at boats out of Central and South America. They're not looking in the right place. A South African registry on a trawler working below the Equator doesn't arouse suspicion. When the South African boat brings its catch to Florida and offloads, she's inspected; the fish are checked in and everything checks out. After thousands of hours on her engines, she goes in for an overhaul—that's when the drugs are offloaded."

Alicia couldn't believe her ears. "If what you are saying is true, wouldn't that cost the cartel too much time and money?"

"The value of the drugs far exceeds the cost of the delay. Keep in mind that no one is suspicious of these boats, not even the other drug interests; security isn't a concern."

"How do you know all this?"

"I have my technology, remember? Also, a journalist started nosing around after her brother died."

"Was murdered," she corrected.

She reached back, blinded by tears and feeling the chair behind her, sank down.

"You're a prick," she snapped as she wiped her tears.

Nemo set his cup upon the table and moved toward her, kneeling next to where she sat. "Am I? Do you think I'm saying this just to hurt you?"

"You're a monster."

Nemo paused, "Perhaps. Yes, I think you are correct in that. Nonetheless, how would you like to deliver justice?"

"Get away from me!"

Nemo stood up and straightened his shirt. "Very well. Fifty miles north of our location, three such trawlers are cruising back to Florida laden with drugs. When they arrive, the fishing they do takes on a whole new definition. I'll be in my quarters if you need me. You can take your breakfast in private."

With that, Nemo unceremoniously piled a bunch of food onto a plate, grabbed a carafe of coffee and walked out.

Alicia began to sob uncontrollably. "No...no. Not my Michael! I miss him so much, he was so good..." she sobbed. She buried her head in her arms on the table and shook silently. After a few moments, she pounded the table, "Nemo, you bastard!"

8

THE MAELSTROM

Nemo sat at the desk in his room, a spartan cell in comparison to the rest of Nautilus' opulence. There on the desk was a photograph of a young woman and two children. On the opposite corner of the desk was a photo of two people just past middle-age, but not yet elderly. All of them looked out with smiles and bright eyes. Nemo stared down at the diary before him. His pen, a fountain pen layered in mother of pearl, lay across the opened blank page. He felt himself at the edge of a great precipice. He could choose to step back or step out, but he knew with the finality of resolution what would happen. Others would say it was fate, but he did not believe in fate, only in decisions and consequences. He had just made a decision by offering her vengeance. If she accepted his offer, he would bear the consequences for her path. Would she master it or would she become as he had?

A light knock on the door brought him out of his reverie. He looked up to see Alicia looking in at him while trying to take in the details of his plain, nearly empty room.

"I'd like to talk to you."

"I'm not in the mood for mind games, Ms. Petit-Smith. If you're going to try..."

"No, no. I mean it. No games. Are you positive of what you said about those boats and the whole drug thing?"

"Yes. I have a report and even before you came aboard, I was intercepting radio traffic for months. I have recorded everything and you can review it, but time is of the essence. At a certain point, I won't be able to intercept them without risking security."

"I understand. Okay, Nemo, I'm going to trust you."

"Very well," Nemo nodded in assent.

"Go change into some clothes and the steward will bring you to the conn."

Nemo pressed a button on his watch. "Battle stations! Silent running!"

The elevator opened and Alicia paused before entering the control room. The numerous rows of gauges and screens and the red lighting took her aback.

"Please, enter. This is the Nautilus' control room or conn for short. From this room the ship takes on a life of its own. It can see, hear, respond; in other words, it is sentient –it is an extension of ourselves."

"How do we find them?"

"We are moving at a rate of 100 knots-that's about…"

"Yes, I know 115 miles per hour; I'm not an imbecile."

"Of course. As I said before, I have been tracking them. They are now just twelve miles away. We shall pass them and wait; at the right moment we shall jam their communications and cut them in half—literally."

Alicia looked at him disbelieving what she heard.

"You can view it on the forward monitor," Nemo added.

Alicia looked to her left and saw an enormous screen that was now blackened. Nemo touched a switch and the three fishing trawlers' propellers were heard over a speaker.

"Noisy machines; they'll never hear us."

"What about their sonar?"

"Unlike where you stumbled over me, we're in deep water and the Nautilus' external covering—skin, I like to call it—absorbs most sonar pings. We won't appear on their equipment. Coffee?" Nemo politely offered. Alicia silently shook her head and wondered at Nemo's coolness.

"It's so detached for you, isn't it? You don't see the people dying on those ships. It's just some sick game— like a video game."

Nemo shot a look at her and his eyes narrowed. "It is not impersonal. I know the faces of my adversaries— as you shall, too."

Nemo reached over and flicked a switch and the previously black screen lit up and displayed a view of the solid blue of the water. A subdued gong sounded to indicate that they were at the determined point of intersection.

"Reduce speed to five knots, then full-stop. Up periscope-display view."

A single bell chimed and a few moments later a picture of three fishing boats moving across the bright blue water emerged on the big screen. One led and the other two ran parallel just behind.

"This is going to be easy. Give close-up 100-times."

Again the single bell toned softly. The faces of the men on deck came into view. They were sweaty and bare-chested. Some smoked cigarettes while others passed a bottle to each other.

"I'm afraid I'm going to have to retract the periscope when we go in. The only view available to you will be just after it's over."

Alicia said nothing; her legs felt weak.

"Look at that," Nemo motioned toward the screen.

One of the men, obviously the captain, was holding up a white brick-shaped object and was pointing to it as the others cheered.

"No doubt about it. Sit down in this chair and put this harness on."

"What? Why?"

"Because we're going to have a collision in a few minutes and unless you want to split your head open on the control panel, you'll do as I say."

Alicia hurriedly fastened the clasps of the shoulder and lap belts. Nemo began to descend the stairs.

"Where are you going?"

"The cockpit. I shall drive the Nautilus myself."

The lights dimmed and less than a minute passed when Alicia felt the forward movement of the Nautilus. She was being pushed back into her seat even though she was tightly harnessed. She felt the bow raise its angle about 10 degrees and then level off. She detected a slight shudder, then nothing. The Nautilus tilted on her side and then the vibration occurred again. The Nautilus plunged forward again, building speed she could feel in her back, when the Nautilus' forward motion was slowed just a bit. Suddenly the screen illuminated and Alicia could see what had taken place.

The first fishing boat's superstructure was just slipping below the surface while the men on board pushed away from her, clinging to whatever debris they could. The second vessel was knocked on her side and looked like a bathtub toy. Men were scrambling up the exposed side of the boat. The last boat was nothing but flotsam with men clinging to bumpers and floats. The Nautilus was cruising toward this last group of survivors and cut sharply as it dove beneath them. The monitor had followed this movement and Alicia could see the vortex that spawned from the displacement of water. Men were clutching and kicking upward, reaching toward the surface and air but could not pull free of the terrible swirling suction. Their still spinning bodies were lost from view when the mangled hull of one of the other fishing vessels filled the monitor. It hung there as though suspended by strings. The Nautilus passed closely alongside and then angled off, the thrust of the propulsion system directly impacted the suspended mass. It flew apart as though something inside it had exploded. Inside the hull, some bodies had been freed and they, too, were washed along the powerful current of the Nautilus' hydraulic propulsion.

Alicia felt the Nautilus descend and then stop. Slowly the vessel tilted back and began to move forward and upward. Alicia sat at nearly a 90 degree angle. The screen showed a small doughnut ringed in light that was growing more distinct every second. It was a life raft and she could see that the Nautilus was going to strike it as a hammer strikes a nail head. As she viewed it growing closer, she involuntarily shielded her eyes. But there was no impact, no sound. Alicia could see the sun through the veils of water near the surface, but then it began to darken as the Nautilus slid backward and then leveled off. The sound of a speaker startled her; it was Nemo.

"Listen to the sound of their pulverized bodies hitting the water."

Just then a grainy static came through the speaker and some dozen small splashes were heard and then the speaker went silent.

Suddenly, DOC appeared in full battle mode. He was an ugly machine with the two extra arms unfolded from his back that arched above the sphere of his head. They were steel bones that tapered at the edges like sword blades and were motivated by powerful electric motors concealed within the body.

"The Captain commands that you join him in the forward salon."

Ordinarily, Alicia would have bristled at being commanded and would have protested, but was at present dissuaded. Alicia looked at him and calculated. There were no pressure points, no soft tissue, no eyes to gouge. It was obvious that anyone attempting a joint lock would literally be shredded. She was overwhelmed and so she simply complied.

Alicia unbuckled herself and slid forward from the chair and sunk down as she tried to stand. Despite her relative physical inactivity, she was exhausted from the ordeal. DOC just stood there and did not assist, as he was in battle mode. A second attempt worked better and before she knew it, she was being conducted into the forward salon. The viewing panels were opened and she saw the floor of the ocean littered with the new debris. Bodies hung at various depths, their faces grotesque in the watery strangulation. Sharks began to cruise around, circling the fresh kill. She was about to turn away when she caught other movement. A diver was working among the wreckage. Another, very large diver appeared alongside him and then she noticed that the second diver was not a human at all, but a robot. The machine lifted heavy pieces of decking and equipment from the vessel as the first diver worked his way into the cabin portion of the vessel. A few minutes later he emerged and both began moving toward the Nautilus and then passed out of view. Alicia helped herself to some water from a self-filling decanter to wash back the wave of nausea rising within her throat.

She paced the room looking out at the sharks which were in a high-pitched feeding frenzy. "Disgusting," she hissed. Alicia could not believe what she had just witnessed. Worse, she couldn't believe that she had agreed to any of this. They were drug dealers, it is true, but to torture and kill is never justified. It was obvious that Nemo was a sadistic maniac and that it was only a matter of time before he would turn on her. Her defense would be weak, futile, but nonetheless valiant, she decided.

The viewing panel suddenly closed and Nemo entered the salon. He appeared much differently than Alicia had previously seen him. He had shaved his beard and his

hair was carefully combed. Instead of his usual navy blue uniform, he wore an absolutely black tunic and pants. The collar of the tunic was deep purple satin as was the
piping on his pants. A simple, black beret sat upon his head. He wore stark white
gloves and he moved toward Alicia very slowly. Taken aback she gaped at him. He
produced a simple, small wooden box varnished black and held it toward her. She
automatically took it from him. He then extended his right arm and offered his hand.
"My sincerest condolences, Alicia Petit-Smith. May he rest in eternal peace and dwell in
light."

Confused, Alicia mechanically looked down at the box and pushed back its lid.
Instantly she put her hand to her mouth and tears began to flow down her cheeks. She
took her brother's watch, his college graduation present from her, and let the box drop
to the carpeting. She turned it over and read the inscription and then pressed the
watch to her cheek, kneeling down and shaking with sobs. Nemo knew all too well the
emotion he was witnessing. He also knew better than anyone the need for privacy, and
so he quietly turned and left her alone.

Alicia did not know what to make of all that happened. Time seemed to stand still
for the dreadful moment, yet there was some release of pent up rage and in that she
took some comfort. She had not stopped staring at the watch. She thought of all those
people she had interviewed whose family members had been murdered and who
disapproved of the death penalty: "This prisoner's death shall not bring back my loved
ones." Certainly, that was true, but still, there was some satisfaction, some dark sense of
accomplishment to have seen the retribution delivered so completely. She looked up to
see the carnage on the ocean floor, but the panels had been closed for some time. She
remembered the steward standing at the corner of the salon.

"How long have the panels been closed?"

"Two hours," came the laconic reply.

"I'd like them opened; I'd like to see the wreckage from the...the incident."

She was embarrassed at having used such a euphemism; it was the very type of
cover-up she loathed in others.

"We are 100 miles from that place, ma'am."

She was taken aback by her lack of discerning the time. She wondered if Nemo
had lost all track of time. She wondered if time for him was nothing more than another
instrument or formula he used to accomplish things, useful for a purpose but not
important in itself.

Nemo was becoming less inhuman, but no less enigmatic. Something about him
now intrigued her at a deeper level. Something told her that he was reaching out, not
from mere sympathy, but that he felt and therefore knew her grief and her anger. She

looked at her brother's watch and turned it over in her hand. He was returned to her, and her eyes welled up afresh.

This act of kindness, this effort to close the wounds, no matter how slight, could not be betrayed.

"I'd like to see Nemo."

"One moment, please. I shall text message the Captain."

A moment later the steward responded.

"The Captain would like to know if you are up to dining with him, but understands if not."

"Yes, I would like to join him. I would like to go to my room to clean up, first."

"I shall convey your response."

9
COMMISERATION

As Alicia entered, she noticed that her room had been redecorated and refurnished. A large writing table had been added with stationery and an assortment of different pens. On her nightstand was a bouquet of flowers, the likes of which she had never seen before. Brilliant yellow and orange anemones, somehow preserved and alive out of water, competed with various textures of white coral to catch the eye. A painting adorned the wall above the dressing table. In it, a nymph, softly colored in fleshy hues, yet armed with a deadly trident, fends off a shark in the midst of a storm as sailors cling to debris from a recent wreck. It was Renoir's lost "Water Fury" seascape.

She opened the wardrobe to change her navy blue blouse which had been damp from her sobbing. To her amazement there was a collection of blouses, skirts, pants, and even a nightgown in what was a superlative form of silk. The colors ranged from deep purples to crimson and various shades of gold. She chose a deep purple blouse and black, well-fitting slacks. The slippers were the same as before, but seemed brand new. The steward appeared at the door.

"Dinner is served in the gallery tonight, ma'am."

"Ah yes, be right there."

Alicia washed her face at the basin and brushed her hair.

As she entered the gallery, Nemo stood from his seat at the table and motioned toward her chair. Instead of the usual long rectangle, the table was a comfortable oblong shape that demanded closer proximity. As Alicia was being seated by the steward, she noticed Nemo seemingly for the first time. He wore a dark navy military style dinner jacket that cut into a small vee about midway down the chest. A white banded -collar shirt with silver buttons shown beneath the tunic.

"How are you?" Nemo asked.

Her reply would have been unimaginable at any time previously, but she sincerely replied.

"Fine and I just want to say thank you. It means a lot."

"It is a hurt that will never heal," Nemo commented. "Sometimes, though, it is a little thing like a watch that anchors our sanity."

The steward began presenting dishes.

"Ah, dinner is served. Are you sure you have an appetite?"

"Very much!" she rejoined.

"Well, then!"

"By the way, I like what you did with my room. The clothes are a little much, though." A slight bead of perspiration appeared on Nemo's brow.

"I have overstepped my bounds—my apologies."

"I like the intention, though. The navy jumpsuits were getting old."

Nemo feigned mirth and asked about the Renoir, "And the Water Fury?"

"Well, that is perfect, right on target!"

A genuine smile beamed from Nemo's face.

"Artwork aside, how did you know that I would agree to everything?"

"We are kindred spirits, Ms. Petit-Smith."

"Alicia," she corrected.

"I know what it is like to have people you love taken away— murdered, butchered!"

His savage tone gave her pause. He stopped short; he had said too much perhaps.

"You know my story," Alicia said softly. "You can tell me if you wish."

Nemo's brow contorted. He motioned as he would speak, but fell silent. He stared off somewhere beyond Alicia, beyond the gallery and the Nautilus, beyond the sea itself.

"I was a defense contractor for the U.S. Navy. My specialty was submarine warfare. I worked on utilizing sodium/hydrogen propulsion systems for submarine use as well as stealth technology. The Navy put me out at a secret location on an atoll in the Pacific. My work was top secret and very exclusive. So exclusive, in fact, that there were no human assembly workers. Everything being assembled was done by robots—the robots that are now my crew.

Nothing is ever totally secret, though, as your own career testifies. Terrorists caught wind of the work being done. They had no way to locate the exact place and really no way to reach it even if they did know it. There are only a few people with my expertise. When the others were accounted for, there was just me. They threatened my family. I had assurances from the Pentagon and NCIS that they'd be safe. They were butchered as they greeted a man whom they thought was me on leave from work.

I knew then that there would be no justice, that the Navy and the police would do nothing definitive. I took what memories I could and returned to work. The government thought I would crack under the pressure. I was required to see a psychiatrist. I had him convinced that my work was for their memory, so the Navy let me keep at it. Well, in a way it was."

"So what happened?"

"Just hours after Nautilus was completed, a terrible accident took place in the sub pen where she would be launched for her sea trials. A power failure shut down the entire facility for a moment and then when it came back on, it spiked, causing extensive damage to the base's surveillance and communications equipment."

"I thought everything was protected from power surges," Alicia suggested.

"Not electro-magnetic pulses from within the facility."

"I see."

"A SEAL team reported to secure the Nautilus. They hadn't planned for DOC, though. Hardened against electronic warfare and impervious to all small-arms fire, DOC went to work and in five minutes it was over.

DOC, along with some of the other units, and I boarded Nautilus and rigged her for launch, storing every supply and every bit of equipment we could fit aboard her. She had not yet been outfitted with much of the equipment that fills the modern submarine. The salon, for instance, was to have housed a fire control station for a new type of guided missile. Neither the weaponry nor the control systems were yet built in. Other similar sections of the Nautilus were wired, but not yet equipped. I would make permanent modifications at a later date in a safe harbor.

The Navy's facility had a nuclear weapon for self-destruction purposes. I hacked into the system and timed it to go off in thirty minutes. The Navy's fail-safe system of destroying and contaminating evidence worked beautifully for me. Any remains, any scraps of evidence of the truth that might exist couldn't be safely handled for at least ten years."

"So, here you are."

"Here I am."

"Are you happy living on the run?"

"I'm no more miserable than I was before. The difference, though, is that I am free. I was cut off from my life. At least beneath the waves I can breathe again. The sea provides for my every need. The clothes we are wearing are made from silk spun by the byssus mollusk. The food we eat comes exclusively from the sea. The medicinal qualities of underwater flora exceed even those of the terrestrial rain forests. It is a dominion to be lived within without destruction. Men bother me, but little."

"The attack we just survived seemed more than just a little bother," Alicia countered.

Annoyed at her comment, Nemo put down the goblet from which he was about to drink and stared at her across the cooling food. His eyes burned a concentrated green, but then softened to their usual light brown.

"Touché. You are correct in your observation. Nothing's perfect; is it? I still know more about the depths than they," he scoffed. "There are places to go where their satellites, sonar buoys, and attack submarines cannot."

"Can't go yet," she corrected. "It's just a matter of time before they find you and counter your technology. And destroy you."

Nemo paused and as he was about to rebuke her, he stopped himself. "I suppose you're right. Ms. Petit-Smith. Something shall be the end of us all," he reflected. "But you needn't worry. You'll be home before that final moment."

She forced a smile and Nemo nodded.

"I have to know," she began, "how did you know about the watch?"

"Ah, the watch, well, yes. The style of the watch, an Omega DeVille, is not the usual choice of the drug mule. It is very expensive, even on your salary, but yet its style is subdued. It exudes elegance, sophistication— and promise."

A tear trickled down her cheek before she realized to raise her napkin.

"I am sorry, Alicia. Have some more champagne, please" and Nemo filled her glass.

"I'm fine, really" she recovered, "this is wonderful champagne. I can't believe you make it yourself."

"I didn't."

"But I thought you use nothing from the land..."

"I raided a sunken yacht off Santorini."

"You what?"

"Well it was already sunk, I simply...liberated it."

Both laughed and began eating. Motioning with her fork she asked, "Did you liberate the pieces in this gallery, too?"

"Trade secrets, Ms. Petit-Smith."

"You are a pirate!" she playfully scolded.

"That's not the word I would have chosen..."

"Of course not!"

"...but I suppose it captures it well enough."

Alicia suddenly lowered her fork and knife and shock spread across her face. "My God. What an awful pun!"

Nemo feigned offense, "Well, we can't all be literary wits."

"No wonder you live at the bottom of the ocean!"

"Yes, that's it," he chuckled, "you see through me."

"Do I?" she asked, suddenly serious.

Nemo looked down at his plate and his brow contracted, "I'm not sure I see through myself at times. I don't always know my way..." He stopped, having said too much. "But, enough of this! How is your dinner?"

"Very good, but rather much. I am very tired."

"Of course," Nemo interrupted, "feel free to retire at any time. Perhaps tomorrow you'd like to stretch your legs a bit and see the world from outside the fish bowl?"

"Diving?"

"Something like that, yes."

"Well if it isn't diving..."

"Alright, already!" Nemo playfully confessed. "We- and that means you, are going plundering. I'm almost out of champagne."

"Right. Till tomorrow, Nemo."

With that Nemo rose as Alicia took her leave and returned to her quarters.

10
PLUNDER!

Entering the salon, wearing her robe over her underwear, her slippered feet padded toward the breakfast buffet. Nemo had been absent-mindedly looking out, observing fish gathering at the expansive observation port when he caught her movement in his periphery.

"You're not dressing?" questioned Nemo.

"Well, we're going diving so I have my underwear on since there was no swimsuit in my closet."

Nemo smiled, "you don't need to wear an uncomfortable bathing suit. We're not wearing the traditional wetsuit."

He took a sip and added, "Besides, at these depths you would be crushed in an instant."

Alicia sat down and nervously bit into a roll. "Oh, nice," she responded.

"Oh, don't worry; you'll be as safe as if you were at sea level."

"Somehow I don't believe you."

"You'll see. Anyway, you should eat heartily. We won't be back on board for a while and you're bound to burn a lot of calories."

He rose and poured himself a cup of coffee to take with him. "Eat up and then put on some sweats. The key is to being comfortable. If your, uh, bra is uncomfortable, leave it behind."

"Wait a minute, Nemo."

"Yes?"

"You're telling me I can wear sweats in this dry suit, but I shouldn't wear a bra?"

As with all the technology aboard Nautilus, Nemo took tremendous pride in the unique dive suits he had designed.

"The suits utilize a kind of pressure neutralization technology that employs a special material called reactive mimetic alloy. Essentially, the material in the suit automatically reacts to external pressure much as a spring would react to pressure being exerted upon it. The difference, though, is that the reactive material resists the pressure at the exact same pressure, thereby creating a neutral balance. It therefore mimics its environment. The alloy has been calibrated to the same sort of pressure felt at sea level."

"So why no bra?"

"Oh, right," Nemo remembered. "The material will be somewhat rigid and quite form fitting. As the suit reacts to the environment, and as it allows for the movement of your diaphragm when breathing, it may cause discomfort for you."

"Yeah, right," Alicia smiled. "I'm going to try to eat now."

"Steward, escort Ms. Petit-Smith to the dive boot when she's ready."

"Yes, sir," came the enthusiastic, programmed response.

"I'll be making final preparations."

As Alicia entered the chamber, she noted the stark difference between the rest of the ship and this area. There was nothing but pale, lime-yellow translucent paint and heavily made fittings and equipment.

"Ah, that was quick. I hope you ate enough."

"Yes, about as much as anyone could, I suppose."

Alicia looked down and her eyes shifted back and forth. Nemo reached out and, for the first time, put a hand on her shoulder.

"You'll be fine. The technology is proven. You really want to see what's there, believe me."

She looked up into Nemo's face and Nemo felt as he did when he placed her back into her bed during the attack when she was suffering from the concussions of the torpedoes. As before, he distracted himself.

"Besides the safety of the suits, I want you to meet a friend of mine."

Nemo turned half way and gestured toward a piece of machinery that Alicia had not noticed before.

"Meet Ulysses. He is an undersea robot that is specially designed to work in deep sea applications. He provides propulsion, protection, and a ready means of communicating with Nautilus. You couldn't be safer in your father's arms."

"Safe, like being with DOC?" Alicia countered.

Nemo turned and looked directly into her eyes, "I left you at breakfast to program Ulysses to safeguard you." Alicia made no reply.

Nemo handed her the dive suit and instructed her on how to put it on. After making sure that her sweatshirt had not rolled onto her back, and that the hood was secure, Nemo folded the two halves of the back together and a very audible hiss emitted as the material closed in upon itself. Ulysses dexterously helped Nemo suit up.

"Well, let's step into the dive boot and be on our ..."

"Aren't we forgetting something?" Alicia asked and pointed to her face, tracing the shape of a mask.

"Oh, no, we don't wear tanks or bother with air lines. We breathe."

"We breathe!?!"

"Yes!" said Nemo with an air of triumph in his voice. "We use a mechanical and chemically operated gill that filters oxygen from the water that our lungs inhale. There is no decompression needed, no dangerous mix of chemicals to avoid intoxication. We breathe!" Alicia just shook her head in disbelief.

"Now, you might be anxious about this, but just breathe slowly and deeply. There is a little bit of drag as the water flows through the gill and the mechanism extracts the oxygen. Deep, relaxed breaths. You'll get the hang of it." Without further delay, Nemo placed straps behind her hood and the mask's soft contours formed to Alicia's face and adhered to the outline of her skin much as a contact lens adheres to one's eye. Below the chin, two wide, bifurcate funnels jutted outward and downward. One pair of vents was for inhalation and the other two were for exhalation. Ulysses performed the same service for Nemo.

The three of them stepped into the dive boot, and Nemo led by example. Sitting on a low bench that jutted from the wall, he put fins on over his feet. Alicia did the same, while Ulysses' eerie, violet eyes glowed, watching the two humans. As if he were addressing a human, he gave a thumbs-up sign and Ulysses closed the hatchway through which they had stepped. Slowly, the robot turned a knob on the wall. A hissing sound of escaping air and penetrating water startled Alicia and she turned toward Nemo with genuine fright in her eyes. Nemo held up his hands with his palms upward and moved them back and forth in the universal "slow-down" gesture. She was trying to breathe fast and shallow, and was fighting the operation of the breathing device. The water was cold and rising past her chest when Nemo thrust out his hand to her. She looked up at him and without taking her eyes off his face, she grasped his hand in a death grip. The line of water worked its way up her mask and then closed over the top of her head.

Alicia felt the terrific cold at first, but then, almost as quickly, it subsided and her body didn't need to shiver to maintain warmth; she began to feel comfortable and her breathing slowed. And then she realized it: she was actually breathing under water! The excitement of this realization brought forth a few shallow breaths which made the mechanism pause in its operation. She remembered Nemo's advice about deep breathing. It was working better and she was in control, and flushed with excitement. She looked over at Nemo who had been watching her the entire time. She nodded in excitement. Nemo withdrew his hand from hers and reached over and pressed a large orange button. Instantly, an oblong opening appeared and Alicia could see the silty bottom. She rushed forward ahead of the others. Ulysses, faithful to his programming, quickly moved out after her and then pulled back from where she tread a few feet above the sea floor. The big robot hovered just behind her and scanned the area for any sharks or other dangers. Nemo gained their position a few seconds later and pointed into the distance. Alicia followed his extended arm and stared into the blue. At first she saw nothing, but slowly a shape began to emerge. It was large and jagged in profile. Nemo touched her arm and motioned toward the back of Ulysses. They both swam over and Nemo opened a small door in the robot's back. Within the small cavity was a joystick and single button. Nemo placed his feet into stirrups that were previously concealed in the robot's sleek sides. He wrapped a Velcro belt around his waist and turning toward Alicia, made a hugging gesture with his arms. She wrapped her arms around his chest and Nemo very slowly pushed the joystick forward.

The robot slid forward, perpendicular to the sea floor and began moving. It was powered by a comparatively miniaturized version of the Nautilus' propulsion system. Water was sucked through venturis and the sodium and hydrogen were separated and used for electric power. Even in fresh water, the system processed electric power from the generator powered by the internal impeller, though without the added power of the sodium. The robot was capable of speed that would easily wash off its passengers. Nemo chose a moderate pace of approximately five knots.

As they pushed through the water, Alicia could feel her dive suit reacting to the increased pressure. As soon as she was aware of some constriction, the suit compensated. She found that she could grip Nemo only so tightly as his suit reacted to the pressure she exerted. She looked over Nemo's shoulder and saw the shape growing in size, and as it did, its shading became more prominent. They were slowing down, but also rising.

It had been a galleon. It was wonderfully intact, even though the port side was collapsed and it listed about thirty degrees. The decking was still present and a single mast still thrust skyward. They circled above and then descended, still circling until they pulled upright at the half buried bow. Nemo rolled his shoulders back as a signal for Alicia to let go which she did while regaining her upright position. Unfastening his Velcro belt, Nemo slid his feet from the stirrups and closed the panel that concealed the joystick. Opening another small panel, Nemo pushed a button and an LCD display began to glow. A few more combinations of buttons started an intricate scan of the area just before them. Nemo pointed at the screen and Alicia saw a number of blips superimposed on the video of the muck bottom before them. At the touch of another button a grid divided the display and flashed. Nemo looked down at the keypad strapped to his left wrist and touched a small red bubble. Instantly, Ulysses moved forward and as he came to an area, an arm extended from his abdomen and penetrated the silt. A moment later the arm pulled out an object and set it carefully next to the hole from which it was drawn. For nearly an hour, Ulysses excavated the field.

Alicia marveled at the robot's efficiency. She recalled viewing footage of unmanned vehicles sorting through wreckage and seizing artifacts from the Titanic. The engineers beamed with pride as their equipment worked through the wreckage. Such child's play! Nemo's robot never faltered, never miscalculated, and uncannily seemed to understand what it was doing.

Just then, Ulysses returned and faced Nemo. Nemo held his right hand before the robot and made a twirling gesture. The robot turned around and Nemo again accessed the panel with the display. As before, he then pressed the red bubble on his keypad. Ulysses sped forward; the jets in his upturned tail section blurred their field of vision as he they churned through the water. As it approached the side of the stricken hulk, the robot slowed as two black tubes unfolded and locked down along the sides of the robot's arms. The robot's propulsion system cut out and it drifted a few yards before losing momentum.

Shafts of laser beamed from the tubes and concentrated their burning points of light at equal points on the galleon's gunwales. Bubbles burst forth as air and debris split from the rotted wood. The intensity of the lasers was making short work of the job as they followed down the side of the ship toward the silt. In only minutes, the vessel would be cut into three sections. Nemo motioned to Alicia and pointed back toward the Nautilus. She looked back into the blue but could see nothing. Nemo then pointed to his keypad which displayed a map and three icons representing themselves and the Nautilus. She gave him the thumbs up and they began their swim back. A half hour later, they were closing the outer hatch of the dive boot.

11
CATHARSIS

As the water drained from the dive boot, Alicia could feel her suit adjusting to the change in pressure. Finally, a green light signaled that the boot was completely drained. Nemo reached behind Alicia's head and unbuckled one of the straps, and then grasped one edge of her mask to break the seal that still held it in place. She reached up and pulled it off the rest of the way. He then did the same with his own mask. As soon as his mask was off, she exclaimed, "Amazing! That's the only word I have for it."

"Yes, it is," came the smug reply. "Now, take it slow, your body will be recovering from the stress or..."

"Oh I feel fantastic. I never thought I'd see anything like..." and as she said this she reached over and punched the big button that had sealed them from the rest of the Nautilus and the hatch opened with a hiss. Nemo watched, amused, as she bounded through the hatchway –and then slid to the floor.

"Whoa! I'm fine. Just a little woozy."

Nemo stepped in behind her, took a deep breath, and hooking his arms under her shoulders, lifted her to her feet.

"Slow down," he chuckled. Then more seriously, he explained. "As effective as the technology is at neutralizing the pressure, the body knows it's not sea level. Your vascular system is still adjusting. Take it slow."

"How deep were we?"

"Three hundred meters," came the reply.

"Three—hundred!?!" "Holy sh..."

"How about some water?" Nemo encouraged.

Alicia just repeated, "Three hundred meters!?!"

Nemo raised his voice and called out, "Steward!"

Seconds later the steward appeared, "Aye, sir!"

"Help Ms. Petit-Smith with her suit and bring her water. Take her to the salon and see that she consumes some carbohydrates."

"Aren't you coming?"

"I have to attend to a few things. Ulysses will be needing orders any moment now."

"What's the next stop? Can I see? You can't just dismiss me after all this!"

"Very well. Ulysses, as effective as he is, needs some help."

Nemo stepped into one of those small alcoves that Alicia had noticed when she first boarded the Nautilus after submerging for the first time. At the small podium within, he flipped a switch and spoke loudly and slowly.

"Ulysses, confirm."

A text message flashed on a small screen: Confirmed.

Crew and sledges en route. Load all items and return home. Signal entry at cargo hatch. Confirm. The screen flashed again the single acknowledgement: Confirmed.

Nemo typed a few commands and then pressed a different keypad on the wall. The screen changed to a view outside the submarine. The view was of the rear portion of the top deck. Suddenly, ten separate hatches opened, and ten domed objects resembling mushroom caps began to emerge. Alicia gave a small gasp of surprise. Uniformly they rose from their channels within the ship and, as at a signal, lifted clear of the deck, leaned forward as Ulysses had done, and sped off toward the shipwreck.

"Ulysses' crew," Nemo announced.

"They aren't as large as he is," observed Alicia.

"No, they aren't equipped with all his location and scanning equipment. Their hydraulics are almost as effective, though, and they can, given the orders, perform a lot of careful, close work. Anything that is damaged won't be from mishandling." Alicia just shook her head.

"Now, Alicia!" Nemo broke her reverie, "I insist. You need to eat and drink or you're going to be in bad shape. Let's go."

Without protest, Alicia submitted to the steward's assistance and shed her suit. She was feeling very fatigued and walked slowly and silently along the corridors. Nemo's pace slackened and he put his hand on her back, the steady pressure of which kept her focused on moving forward. Once they entered the salon, she finally spoke.

"I'm famished."

"Please, eat. It's better you take nourishment this way and get everything functioning properly than having to do an I.V."

She sat down and drank long from a goblet of water and fully exhaled after she finished, "Nothing ever tasted so good." Nemo smiled. Without a further word, they both began eating.

12
PIRATES AND ANTIQUARIANS

Alicia awoke in her bed, still wearing her sweatsuit. It was the first time she had slept without being terrified awake, gasping for air in the drowning vision of the nightmare. Aware of this, she lay there, thinking. She thought about what that night-mare meant. She remembered Ulysses excavating the sea floor and then cutting through the galleon. She was starting to realize what must have happened. The bruises on her body told a story of being pinned by hurled equipment and a collapsing hull, all as the insidious water rose and seeped into her struggling lungs. This she deduced, rather than remembered. Ulysses must have freed her from the tangled metal. Cold sweat beaded on her forehead and she clutched the blanket. Instinctively, she turned to where her own clock would have been on her nightstand in her bedroom back in D.C. One irritating aspect of the Nautilus was that there were no clocks outside of the alcoves and the control center. Then again, does time really matter when you're by yourself at the bottom of the ocean?

She reflected on the galleon and its counterpart, the Nautilus. Both occupied the same element at the same moment. What was the difference between them but several hundred years? The ancient crew had long since stopped living. The Nautilus' crew had never quite been living. Two people stood at the brink of the past and future, and that was a small space called the present. The pressure they resisted wasn't so much the three hundred meters of water. "Three hundred!" she marveled out loud. No, she resolved, it was the pressure of time they felt.

She felt grimy and a little chilled from sweating. She decided to shower and put on some fresh clothes. She was anxious to see what was going on, so she settled for the shower in her room. The water and lather refreshed her and as she dried, she carefully patted the towel around her bruises. Yes, "the incident," as he had called it. She thought to herself that this would be another topic of dinner conversation. And then she stopped and faced the mirror over her wash basin. She realized that she was looking forward to that conversation, but not because she would be told what happened, but because Nemo would be telling her what happened. This twinge of realization was interrupted by another, perhaps more pressing realization—her stomach sharply growled with hunger. She smiled and turned toward the wardrobe.

After dressing in a pair of lightweight pants, long-sleeve tee shirt and the usual soft boots, she checked herself in the mirror. She put her hair back using a very elegant and much too dressy pearl studded comb that was lying on her table. She exited into the corridor and was greeted by the steward.

"Ma'am," the steward came to attention.

"I would really like some breakfast and to see Nemo."

"The Captain instructed me to escort you when you were ready. He is in the laboratory sorting and cataloguing the artifacts."

"Can you bring me breakfast there?"

The steward asked her to wait as he checked with the Captain. A few seconds later the robot repeated the positive message. "What should you like?"

"Oh, pancakes, fruit, and yes, who could live without coffee?"

"Very good, ma'am. Please follow me."

As the steward preceded Alicia into the room, Nemo, wearing a loupe and a doctor's lighted examination band, looked up from the small chain he had been examining.

"Well, good morning, or I should say, good afternoon."

"How can anyone tell in this place?" Alicia chided.

"Touché. Well, you've been down for the count for nearly fifteen hours, so...good afternoon."

"Are you serious?"

"Yes, you fell off to sleep at the table. But don't worry; I finished your dinner so you're still a member in good standing with the clean plate club."

"You're a dork."

"Ah, but a rich dork."

"Well Captain No-Beard, what did you haul in?"

Nemo stared at her hair.

"What, what are you looking at?"

"Nice comb, Senora."

Alicia's hand instantly went to her hair and she pulled out the comb.

"Sixteenth century, Spanish," added Nemo.

Alicia examined the comb as though she never saw it before.

"Oh, my god—this is beautiful!"

"Of course, your first thought was that it was too gaudy or overdressed, but would simply have to do."

Alicia looked sheepishly at him, but then her eyes suddenly fired with resentment,

"It's Senorita, Senor!" They both laughed at the exchange. The steward brought in Alicia's breakfast, and as Alicia ate, Nemo explained what had transpired.

"Some of the galleon's decking had collapsed on Ulysses as he was probing a large deposit of silt in the forecastle."

"Is he alright?" Alicia asked with genuine concern for the robot that she was certain had pulled her from her wreckage.

"Of course he's alright—he is a robot, you know."

"You know what I mean," Alicia responded, not quite knowing what she meant.

"Yes, he broke his way free quite easily. The problem, though, is that it stirred up quite a bit of sediment, slowing down the process. What had been uncovered was now under several inches of silt again. The old galleon's ghosts wouldn't give up their treasure."

"Did you actually find human remains?"

"Yes."

"What did you do with them?"

"After the excavation, I had a grave dug and then I personally placed the remains in the grave. They are buried, quietly and peacefully as they deserve."

Alicia looked hard at this man who thrilled in the obscene carnage of bodies just a couple days ago who also holds memorial services at the bottom of the ocean. Nemo didn't wait for her to respond with what would be an awkward reply.

"Let me show you what we have."

Nemo stepped down from the stool he had been perched on and walked over to a long, well lit area that contained a couple hundred different dilapidated crates and barrels, all soaking in tanks of water.

"If we expose them to the air at once, they would decay immediately and give off such gases as to burden the air purification system. I'll need to finish the process later."

"Where?"

"I have a place that is more suited, but you'll be back home by then." Alicia nodded absently, but her brain spun with thought: He must have a port or base that he goes to from time to time. It must be at the surface or if it is below the surface, it must have a large, open area or at least feature a powerful ventilation system. He kept talking about her departure as imminent, prior to his visiting the secret location. Even the information about such a facility's existence could prove helpful for the U.S. Navy— and she would be the only one to break the story! Alicia's heart jumped at this realization.

"Of course, the comb is yours, but is there anything else you would like?" Nemo had not noticed her preoccupation.

"Sorry?"

"Any other artifacts interest you?"

"Oh, sorry, I spaced out; I need to eat."

"Of course, take your time. None of this is going anywhere. Why don't we go back to the salon? Taking meals in a lab isn't the most pleasant experience," he suggested.

"Oh, okay."

"Don't forget your comb."

"Right—thanks again." Nemo smiled at her and she turned away.

13
UNINVITED GUESTS

As they walked toward the salon, Alicia thought not only of her future, but Nemo's. Their discussion about his inevitable destruction would certainly come sooner with her information. Her observations about the Nautilus' capabilities would render tremendous insight for counter-technologies. Interrupting her thoughts, a klaxon rang throughout the ship and a mechanical voice repeated, "Unidentified vessels! Unidentified vessels!" Nemo sprinted ahead to the nearest alcove and immediately issued orders: "Battle mode! Silent running!" DOC appeared at the end of the corridor. "Move to the conn!" Nemo shouted at him. Nemo raced up several ladders with Alicia not far behind.

Once in the conn, Nemo began activating several screens. He fixated upon one in particular.

"What is it?" Alicia asked in a loud voice.

"Shhh! Keep it down!"

"Well?"

"Give me a minute." The text messages on the display gave a fairly complete picture:

Two vessels, one approximately 1000 tons; one approximately 3000 tons. Range: 10 miles. Speed: 12 knots. ETA: 47 minutes.

Nemo reached over and pushed a button that transmitted the sound of their distant propellers; he then turned a dial to amplify it.

"Noisy, very much industrial and not too subtle."

"What does that mean?"

"It means it's not military unless there are airborne sub-hunters aboard—and that's always a possibility. Still, it's pretty unlikely. In any case, we need to leave before they get too close. There's a good possibility that they are after that galleon. If so, in about five miles they'll start pinging like hell to find it."

Nemo spoke into a microphone: "Maintain silence. Prepare for speed course."

"So where are we headed?"

"I'm not sure. I was hoping to take you back to a civilized port before this, but I think we'll be heading to port ourselves, first. I hope this isn't too inconvenient?"

A week ago this would have been absolutely unreasonable and Alicia would have been suspecting the very worst in treatment. Now, though, it was one more excursion and it provided her with an opportunity for reconnaissance.

"Fine. As long as I can get some breakfast around here."

"Yes, yes," Nemo responded with impatience as he turned toward the steward keeping sentinel at the edge of the room. "Steward, take Ms. Petit-Smith to the salon and give her whatever she wants to eat." The robot's eyes flickered once as he maintained his silence.

Alicia polished off another slice of key lime pie, or what passed for it with the ingredients at hand. Still, it was quite good. She wondered how she would go about ascertaining their position and the location of Nemo's secret port. There were no maps about and no discussion of courses set. She broke up the remaining crust on her plate with deliberate, slow divisions with her fork. Each section separated from the larger piece and then crumbled. Suddenly, she felt uncomfortable in the brightly lit, large room.

"I'll be in my room; I'm tired," she announced.

"I shall communicate this to the Captain," the steward responded briskly.

Alicia closed the door behind her and threw herself upon the bed. She reflected on the advanced technology and the simple, fragile world that she would be instrumental in destroying. But Nemo was a fugitive administering his own form of vigilante justice; he was a killer and had to be brought to justice. She consoled herself with the knowledge that he brought this upon himself. She closed her eyes briefly and tried to shut out any further thought on the matter.

A moment later she sat upright and stared ahead. Expressionless and without averting her eyes, she reached into her pocket and brought out her brother's watch. The stainless steel bracelet felt cold for only a moment as the heat and sweat of her palm brought it to life. The automatic mechanical movement had been wound just enough to send the sweep hand gliding around the dial. She looked down at the bright, ticking thing and wiped her eyes on her sleeve. She held it closer to her face and slowly worked the crown until it tightened. She leaned over and lay on her side.

It wasn't so simple, though. She thought of her brother and she thought of Nemo, and as she did, she felt again his empathy as he had handed her the black box containing the watch. Alicia remembered her decision not to betray Nemo's gesture. Wasn't she culpable in the deaths of those men to some degree, and did she not enjoy some vindication for her brother's sake? She brought the watch to her ear and listened to the mechanism beating within. No, Nemo's execution was inevitable. His fate, like a spinning coin on a table top, needed no help from her to find its point of lost momentum and ultimate failure. It would topple over, she concluded, and so would he. The U.S. Navy would have to rely upon intelligence other than hers. This deliberation worked upon her soul, but finally, her eyes squeezed out the last of her tears under the crushing weight of a troubled sleep.

14
DEAD RECKONING

Alicia woke with slow recognition of her surroundings. She looked out from eyes that took in her surroundings as if seeing them for the first time. She glanced at the watch still clutched in her hand. Three hours had passed since she wound it. She sat up, wiped the dried smears on her cheeks, rose, and walked to her wash basin. She washed her face and brushed back her hair. She put the watch on her wrist and snapped the bracelet closed. It was still much too large for her wrist. The watch, now pendulous, swung to the bottom of the metal loop dangling on her wrist. But she didn't care; it's ill-fit only emphasized the current situation. She opened the door of her room expecting to see the attendant robot, but the corridor was abandoned.

She walked to the salon and entering, noticed a plume of white smoke above a high- backed chair, and then she whiffed the aroma of one of Nemo's cigars. She strode over to the permanently stocked tray of cigars and cigarettes. Choosing a cigarette, she approached Nemo's chair, "Sending smoke signals?" Nemo looked up at her and she held out her cigarette to indicate that she needed a light.

"Oh, of course. I tend to take the lighter with me."

"That's understandable." She pulled up a chair opposite his.

"No observatory today?"

"No, at this speed the panels would cave in and we would flood."

"Where are we headed?"

"Port."

"Really? Yours or mine?"

"Ours. I was going to head back to port after your departure, but it would be more secure to head in for modifications first. As I said before, I hope you don't mind the delay."

"No, that's fine. Of course, if the quality of the food deteriorates or you run out of cigarettes, you could have a mutiny on your hands."

Nemo ignored her attempt at humor; he didn't want to soften the conversation. "You know, I hesitated in even telling you about its existence because I was afraid of being discovered after your return to the world above."

Alicia's face colored intensely as indignation rose hot in her latest conviction to shield Nemo from the more imminent demise she had once contemplated. "You, you think I would actually tell them..." Nemo cut her short with a raised hand.

"If you didn't tell willingly, they'd get it from you through some other means. Trust me on this." As he said this, the glow of his cigar intensified as he drew through it. "You've already seen too much of my world," he exhaled through his nose. Alicia motioned as to speak, but Nemo kept on talking.

"No, you have complete freedom on the ship. You want to see the maps, the rest of the crew, the equipment rooms— it's all there for you. You are right regarding the future. They will eventually find me and destroy me. This brush with the souvenir seekers brought that home to me."

"You mean about airborne hunters?"

"Yes. I know all these variables, yet I never think to consider their impact in terms of how total and complete it could be. It's always a matter of weighing probabilities and finding gaps in other people's reasoning. If not the Navy, then some ridiculous accidental discovery," Nemo trailed off "—like your own."

Alicia listened and stared hard at this enigma sitting before her. Was he departing the field? Was he planning some suicidal run into the side of a reef? If he were, he wouldn't be so eager to modify the Nautilus. Just because he recognized his inevitable destruction didn't mean that he thought it was imminent. Nemo pointed toward the watch hanging off her wrist.

"You want me to adjust that for you so it fits properly?"

"No, I like it as it is."

"Yes. Of course. I understand."

There was no doubt in Alicia's mind that Nemo did, indeed, understand and that his words weren't an empty gesture.

"I appreciate that," she replied. Nemo nodded. Alicia then added, "I would, however, like to know the time so I can set it."

Nemo smiled, for he understood the significance in this seemingly insignificant action. She wasn't just setting a watch; she was setting her own time, her own place.

"Well, would you like to see where we're headed?"

"Well, yeah!" she beamed.

They snuffed out their remaining smokes and Nemo walked over to a large, rather nondescript watercolor of a storm-tossed ship and he distinctly said the words, "Map. On." The painting faded and an LCD map of the Southern Ocean appeared. A small blip appeared and Nemo pointed at it. "This is the Nautilus and we're headed here, just five miles off the Antarctic Peninsula." At Nemo's words, a thin line appeared at the destination. The line was faint and not much larger than the blip that signified the Nautilus.

"What is that line?" Alicia asked.

Nemo tapped the screen and a detailed survey of the area appeared on the screen.

"This is a slight rift in the seabed. The depth is 1500 meters, well out of the diving range of military submarines. This rift is an ancient volcanic vent. The vent itself is only 50 meters wide and 30 meters high. Currents swirl about it and create a treacherous cross current. It's tough navigation, to say the least. Once in, the vent leads down and then slowly upward and empties into a caldera that is some three miles in width. There is open air. The vaulted ceiling stretches some four hundred feet above. In fact, it is the bottom of the Antarctic continent."

Alicia stood, mouth agape. "We're going into this thing?"

"Yes," Nemo enthusiastically responded.

"What do we need to do, anyway?"

"Ah, yes, the modifications. You know how you were able to track me in the Persian Gulf? Well, as I thought about the vulnerability of being in shallow, warm water, I thought, 'what if I were able to manufacture cold deep water at will?'"

Alicia looked at him and waved her hand dismissively.

"You know, you were better as a scientist and not a mad scientist."

"No really, it's quite simple. This remnant of the late Cretaceous contains minerals and elements unknown to science, at least science at sea level. On one expedition to this subterranean caldera, I found amazing quartzes and unknown elements. One of these I have found to exude intense cold when subjected to saltwater. Amazingly, the effect does not lessen as long as the salinity of the water remains constant."

"How did you know this?" Alicia asked with genuine amazement at this discovery. "Well, I'd like to say that I had a complicated hypothesis in mind, but the fact of the matter is that I knocked it off a table in the lab and as I reached to catch it, I knocked over a beaker of saline solution that spilled over it. As I was cleaning up the broken glass, I picked up the piece and then dropped it immediately. It was so cold I suffered contact burns."

"That's amazing!"

"I can incorporate this into the Nautilus' ballast system to give the appearance of deep, cold water to help baffle active sonar."

Alicia averted her eyes and said nothing in response.

"What are you thinking?"

"I was just thinking that it's too bad that this couldn't be put to better use than to keep you hidden. I mean this could have implications for global warming, preserving endangered species, all kinds of things."

"Well, let them discover it for themselves!" Nemo snapped. " I'm out of the collegiality business."

He brushed past Alicia and strode out of the salon. Alicia crossed her arms and stared at him as he left; she sighed in impatience as he disappeared around the corner. "Worse than a child," she mumbled to herself. She returned to the tray of cigarettes, selected another one, and quickly lit it. She threw herself into one of the wing chairs, and after a few contemplative puffs, began to reconsider Nemo's behavior.

She was beginning to understand Nemo's vulnerabilities and limitations. Her first impulse would have been to dismiss him as being a megalomaniac, an egomaniac, or even just a prima donna. His anger and the grudge he held could easily be justified, though. He had been used by the military-industrial complex; his family had been wiped out; his only recourse, as he saw it, was to salvage what was left of his life: the Nautilus. Still, his moments of empathy with others' grief made his bloody behavior incomprehensible and unjustified.

As she flicked an ash into one of the numerous shell ashtrays scattered about, she felt the substantial weight of her brother's watch, and it tugged at her conscience. She couldn't quite condemn Nemo without condemning herself, a prospect which she didn't care to think about at the moment. She distracted herself by focusing on the current agenda of traveling to a lost time in an unknown part of the planet, a part that probably would never be known. She left the salon and headed toward Nemo's room to learn when they would arrive.

His door was closed, so she knocked softly. Again there was no response. She gently turned the handle and entered. The room was empty. She looked about at the sparse furnishings. A simple, twin-sized bed stood near one wall. His desk was plain and uncluttered, with a row of photographs neatly grouped in one corner. Intrigued, she walked over for a closer look. It was obvious that this had been his family.

In one photo, two people past middle-age, but not yet elderly, warmly smiled. The strong jaw line of his father and his mother's eyes were clearly recognizable in their son. Another picture featured Nemo's two children, who were about eight and ten years old. Faces posing silly for the camera looked out from behind thin glass and time. "Cute," Alicia uttered. She then saw the photo of their mother, his wife.

She picked up the picture and took in every feature. It was an elegant black and white portrait of a woman in her prime, smiling and confidently defined by the chiaroscuro of the photo. Though a close-up, Alicia could tell that she was petite, but nonetheless had strong bone structure. Her eyes were expressive and the brows arched slightly in a playful mood. There was a joy of living that shone through that image on paper, and it was easy to see how he could love her. Under other circumstances they all would have been friends, perhaps. But not now. Not ever. Alicia carefully replaced the picture to its place among the dead, among the living memories of the man, and quietly closed the door behind her.

15
Safe Passage

Alicia found Nemo in the conn absently pouring himself a cup of coffee while staring intently at a paper map and then quickly looking up an LCD display.

"How's it going?" she interrupted. "When do we arrive?"

Nemo looked up and smiled, "Soon. Next stop, the Cretaceous, excepting a few high-tech pieces of equipment."

"Really?" Alicia enthusiastically asked.

"We'll be at the opening of the rift in fifteen minutes. At that point we're going to stop just outside and send a probe in to make sure we can still access the inner caldera. It is, after all, a present day, shifting tectonic plate. This might be a trip for naught."

"Were you going to tell me at all?"

"I thought you might be sleeping, and I didn't want to disturb you. Frankly, there's nothing to see in the vent. It's a dangerous place with very intricate navigation. One small mistake could make this tunnel our tomb.

In fact, I don't even pilot the Nautilus. The probe will send back data about the passage; we'll weigh our chances and, if it looks like a 'go,' the navigational computers will take us through. The salon will be sealed, as well as all bulkheads. The crew will be on standby in search and rescue mode and we'll be holed up in here. The only other open area will be the cockpit below us, so I can control the ship if there is failure of any of the components in the conn."

"To be honest," Alicia admitted, "I'm more excited than worried."

Nemo smiled, "You're starting to understand what I see living this way. There are risks, to be certain, but the excitement of exploration and the constantly changing, living environment transcends those dangers. In some way, the thought of succumbing to those dangers within the environment is less terrifying than those dangers from above the surface."

"How so?"

"Well, look at it this way. If you are swimming and you are attacked by a shark, you have no complaint of injustice. You are in his environment, his element, and you appear as either a threat or a source of food. Some violent thrashing, major blood loss, shock, and death. That's it. No one could say, 'this was unjustified', 'this was unexpected'. Even the person being attacked can't wonder why this could happen.

It's the most natural thing in the world. I could never understand public expression of astonishment when an orca at Sea World would occasionally nip or otherwise bully one of the trainers. This is a highly intelligent animal that is at the apex of predators. Doing circus tricks in a fishbowl isn't natural. Taking instruction and basking in the praise of a creature that, though resembling your favorite prey, can't even swim fast or deep has to be tiresome. What do we expect?"

"I see your point," Alicia countered, "but what if the attacks from above are justified?" Nemo's eyebrows arched. Before he could respond a gong chimed.

"We'll continue this conversation later," he quickly said, "we've just arrived outside the rift. We need to deploy the probe."

Nemo turned his attention to an unlit screen as he took a walkie-talkie from a holster fastened to the side of one of the consoles. He pushed a blue button that was on the top of the same console. After a few moments, he spoke into the walkie-talkie to confirm that the probe was, in fact, online.

"Ulysses, prepare for geographic danger assessment and navigational plot."

"Affirmative," returned a mechanical, deeply toned voice.

"Signal when all systems are ready."

"All systems, ready."

"Prepare to exit dive boot."

"Prepared."

Nemo quickly tapped out a combination of keystrokes on the console's keypad and instantly a screen displayed a diagram of the Nautilus, and through colorfully illuminated animations, showed the action taking place. A miniature figure emerged from the deck well aft of the conn. As soon as the robot cleared the dive boot, the previously unlit screen flicked on.

"We're seeing what he sees. From this point until he returns to the Nautilus, every aspect of his reconnaissance will be recorded. Computers onboard will crunch numbers and a course will be plotted."

"How long will all this take?"

"It's not an exact science right now. It could be an hour or it could be two hours."

A grid of statistics was now superimposed at the corner of the screen showing the real time feedback of the robot's observations.

"Right now he's encountering cross currents of twenty knots," explained Nemo, "he is having to gradually tack his way in. By turning into the currents, at least for the most part, his intakes, now force fed, enable his propulsion system to operate more efficiently and more powerfully. With some careful rudder, he'll be in the vent in a few minutes. A human swimmer, no matter how capable, would have been either washed away from the vent or dashed upon the sharp lava rock debris surrounding the vent."

Alicia marveled at how powerful Ulysses had been built and how thoroughly designed. At that moment the screen changed hues to blue, green, and violet splotches.

"What's happening?" she asked.

"We're getting video feed in infrared." Nemo depressed the button on the walkie-talkie and spoke: "Schematic view."

"Affirmative," came the swift reply.

The screen changed again to reveal a black and white schematic of what the robot was perceiving. All the while a crawl at the bottom of the screen flowed with numbers punctuated by decimal points. These were the several thousand measurements and calculations being taken every second.

"Right now, Ulysses is going to proceed at a very slow pace, almost walking speed. We need to be sure because rushing through it might provide an incomplete picture."

"What's the current like now?" Alicia inquired.

"It's steady at fifteen knots, but not turbulent, which is good news for us."

"How long will this take?"

"Patience..." Nemo began, but was immediately interrupted.

"Yes, yes, it's a virtue," Alicia held up her hands in protest, "and I realize that this could take a couple hours. How long will it take him to scan the tunnel and what comes after that?"

Nemo reached over and tapped a computer mouse. "He'll be done with the tunnel in forty-five minutes and then pass through to the port itself. It depends, of course, on what he finds. If everything is as I last left it, we'll be taking him back on board within seventy-five to ninety minutes. Why, what's your hurry? Do you have an appointment?"

"Very funny." Alicia smiled and began to pace. "This is just so exciting! I'll be seeing things no one has! I just wish I were educated in geology. I won't be able to appreciate what I'm seeing."

"I understand," Nemo sympathized. "I've come across so many things that are out of my depth."

"Please, you're killing me with these puns!"

"Hmm? Oh, depth. I didn't even think of that. Bad humor comes so naturally for me. Really, though," he continued, "there are creatures of which the rest of the world has only caught glimpses. The colossal and giant squids, for example. I've..."

"You've seen them!?!" interrupted Alicia.

"Yes, I've observed them feeding ...and being fed upon. They are a special type of cephalopod and I think the folks at the various research agencies are going about their studies all wrong. You can't use floodlights with them. Their eyes are the size of dinner plates and the lights are just overwhelming. You have to use different technologies. Also, they send down unmanned vehicles that dangle there for a few hours and are then brought up. No animal is going to go near it. It needs to stay there in an inconspicuous place and become part of the environment before the surrounding life will ignore it."

"Sounds pretty obvious to me," Alicia responded.

"Some of the best insights are the most ordinary observations," Nemo concluded. "What can I expect to find in this port of yours?"

"Well, it's going to look like every artist's rendering of hell. It's pitch dark, smells a bit of sulfur, and the vaulted ceiling amplifies sound in a manner that is truly amazing. Every sound, from the movement of water to falling rocks, sounds like doomsday."

"How shall we see?"

"I have set up a lighting system that utilizes some special, large quartz crystals that, when charged with electricity at the right cycle, will illuminate about a half mile area."

"There are tides within the caldera," continued Nemo. "The rotation of the earth along with the hobble of it on its axis creates tides on a four hour cycle. We'll park the Nautilus on a basalt shelf at high tide, anchor her securely, and when the tide rolls out, we'll get to work." At that moment a chime sounded. "Over," Nemo spoke into the walkie-talkie.

"Captain, the scan is complete. Navigational success is approximately 92.753%."

"Affirmative. Return to Nautilus at full speed."

"Aye, sir."

"Well, this shouldn't be a problem," Nemo concluded. "Once we get into the caldera, and if the tide is out, I suggest we eat a good meal and be prepared for a long period of work."

"What can I do?" asked Alicia.

"You'd be best off exploring the area. As you have said, you'll never see this again." Almost as an afterthought, Nemo added, "There's nothing alive down here, at least on land."

"What?" Alicia's smile suddenly faded.

"Well, sometimes the sonar picks up movement within the lake and the pinging is sea life of course...big sea life at that."

The color now drained from her face. "Are you serious?"

"Of course. I never joke about these matters. Look, if Ulysses can manage his way into the caldera, possibly a whale, whose sonar is intuitive, would be able to enter."

"You've seen these whales?" Alicia intensely asked.

"No, it's just a hypothesis of mine."

Alicia's head was swimming with every lousy sci-fi B movie she had ever seen. Nemo seemed to read her thoughts. "No, I doubt there are any Jurassic creatures left over. There probably are some unique life forms that thrive in this otherwise inhospitable environment, at least at the cellular level."

"Right," she said assuringly, more for her own benefit than in response to Nemo.

A little later, a gong softly sounded and Nemo depressed a button on the console. "Ulysses is back and boarding," Nemo announced. "Once locked down, we'll begin moving through the vent."

"I wish we could see out as we go," Alicia regretted.

"The slightest touch to the observation panels could be disastrous. The best we can safely manage is to watch an animation of our progress."

Alicia sat on a stool that swung out on an arm attached to one of the consoles. Nemo typed at one of the keyboards in silence. Alicia turned away and looked at the watch dangling from her wrist.

Alicia still couldn't believe what was happening to her, both in circumstance as well as within herself. She was caught up in the adventure and novelty, and she knew it. She shuddered inwardly when she thought of the murders she had agreed to. What was worse was the realization of her relief and almost happiness afterwards which she had somehow registered as justice. She was becoming as corrupt as Nemo, but suffered no apparent transformation. She chided herself for her naiveté, as though she would somehow physically change like Dr. Jekyll's Mr. Hyde. She looked over at Nemo whose profile was now clearly drawn. He was intent, academic, if not banal. His newly shaved look enhanced his jaw line. When he smiled, he betrayed a dimple which added somewhat of a youthful appearance at lighter moments. When he didn't smile, his brow cast a shadow, and his face seemed expressionless.

She was doing it again, somehow connecting with this enigma that could kill at one moment and joke at the next. At first she admired his creation, now she was noticing the finer points of his appearance. Alicia told herself that it was her training as a journalist to note details and that was all, no more to it than that—it just had to be.

Nemo interrupted her thoughts by updating her on their progress, which now seemed to Alicia to have flown by. "We'll be through the vent in fifteen minutes. According to my calculations, we'll emerge in the caldera at just half-past low tide. In two hours we'll be able to anchor, set the skids and get down to work."

"Sounds good," Alicia laconically replied.

"In fifteen we'll eat a good meal and I'll go through a map and a few precautions for your exploration."

The mention of the exploration brought a smile to Alicia's face; she had nearly forgotten all about it even as she questioned her own emotions over the situation.

A very few minutes later, the Nautilus began its ascent at a thirty degree angle and after a few moments, eased to ten degrees and then, exhausting the last bit of momentum, broke the surface.

16
The Best Laid Plans

"I thought you said that there were only whales," Alicia said, her voice rising. They were discussing Alicia's upcoming exploration over dinner in the salon.

"Yes, of course, most likely, but what if you were to slip into the water or get caught by the incoming tide and there were...well, more than just whales?" Nemo challenged.

"Like what?"

"Sharks."

"So the dive suit would save me from the jaws of a large shark?" Alicia countered.

"Definitely, provided he doesn't grab your head."

"Well, in any case, I don't want to wear that thing on shore. It's like an iron lung or something when not submerged."

"I understand, Alicia, but believe me when I tell you that down here the best laid plans can go awry. When the tsunami hit in 2004," Nemo explained, "the force initially disturbed the tides of the caldera, and I was caught by the high surf of one premature tide and was dashed into the rocks. If it weren't for the dive suit, I would have broken my back. Even the suit was dented and damaged to where Ulysses had to cut it off me once we were back aboard. I was bruised for weeks." Nemo paused and looked down at his goblet of water and added, "Also, there are—shadows."

"What are you talking about?" Alicia demanded.

"I don't exactly know. As I said, it's pitch black and where the ring of light ends, it's like the terminator line on the moon; it's just black water. As dark as it is, I have seen shadows rising and then falling, sometimes several just outside the line of light. I have sent Ulysses down with video and non-invasive observation technologies. There was no sign of anything. As soon as he was back aboard, they would appear again. I once tried to take video from one of the Nautilus' observation posts built within the hull, but as soon as I began recording, the shadows disappeared. It's as though they knew what I was up to. I'm a scientist, but it set my hair on end. It was creepy, but even more than that, something, I felt..."

"Dread," Alicia finished his thought.

"Exactly," Nemo responded, "thank you."

"It's the Problem of Pain," began Alicia, "C.S. Lewis describes the difference between being scared of something in the physical realm—a tiger in the next room—and the dread of something supernatural, like a ghost in the next room."

Nemo stared into Alicia's eyes and seemed to be looking through the back of her head at something behind her. "Ghosts?" Nemo mouthed the word. His brow furrowed and his lips parted as though he were about to say something further but then stopped. Time stopped like the final brush stroke of a portrait's frozen pose. His stare retraced itself from looking through her eyes to looking into her eyes, and then he glibly passed off the awkwardness, "I suppose ghosts makes for a satisfactory answer when the facts are unknown." He picked up his fork and quickly ate another scallop, chewing quickly and swallowing it half whole. "I was thinking more along the lines of a six gill shark. They get to be about twenty feet long and live at these depths. I don't know how dangerous they can be, but you are going to wear that dive suit."

Alicia chewed her piece of grouper and nodded her head in the affirmative. The shadows of which Nemo spoke were creepy, but the idea of sharks was real enough to don the suit and move about protected, albeit uncomfortably. Nemo rose from the table. "Excuse me, but I need to attend to a few things. When you're done, you can make your way back to the conn and we'll be ready to pilot the Nautilus in."

"Yes, of course, Nemo," Alicia replied.

After taking his leave, Nemo walked briskly back to his room. After entering, he closed the door, locked it and made his way to the table with the photographs of his family. He picked up the picture of his children and pressed the cold glass to his cheek. "My little ones!" he sighed and tears ran from beneath his tightly creased eyelids. He reached out toward the other photographs but did not touch them. "Gone—all gone!" Nemo sank to his knees and leaned forward until his face touched the rubber decking. "The best laid plans... I killed them. I killed them by not stopping when I could have. If I hadn't kept on with the work...." Tears came hard as he fought back sobs for breath. For five minutes he kept on this way until exhausted, and he lay on his side panting. A chime on his watch broke the rhythm of his labored breathing. The steward was summoning him. "Yes?"

"The passenger wants to know if everything is alright and if you are still planning to meet her in the conn."

"Yes. Fine. Be there in a few minutes." Nemo collected himself, stood, and walked to the mirror over his washstand and rinsed a washcloth and wiped the smears from his face. Just as he brushed his hair back with his hand and was about to leave, he caught the reflection of his stand of photographs on the table. He paused, took a deep breath, and proceeded to the door and exited.

17
MOORING

As Nemo made his way up the stairs, Alicia's voice greeted him before he could see her. "It's about time!"

Nemo made his best effort at wit. "Patience is..."

"But not now!" Alicia playfully shouted over him. As she caught sight of him, she paused. "Everything okay?"

"Yes, perfectly fine."

"It's just..."

Nemo cut her off without directly looking at her. "Fine. Let's open the hatch and shed some light on this world." Nemo led the way up the steep stairs and the hatch slid open. Both Alicia and Nemo crowded into the rounded cubbyhole of the sail. Nemo reached underneath and touched a pad that instantly produced a red glow at their feet, illuminating the space. Alicia began to cough. "The air... it isn't!"

"Do you want some oxygen?"

She gave a few more coughing grunts and shook her head no.

"Take it easy. Breathe slowly." Nemo put his hand on her back in the way people do who try to help the one choking by sympathizing more than rendering any actual physical assistance. All the same, it seemed to work; she began to breathe easier. Nemo's hand lingered for a moment more than necessary and when he realized this, he pulled it back as though he had been scalded. Alicia looked at him as he brought his watch toward his face and depressed one of the buttons and spoke, "Make way to anchorage and activate all spotlights and underwater lights. Commence!" Instantly, the Nautilus was ablaze with bluish white xenon light. Slowly the vessel was crossing the blackness. Looking over the side of the sail, Alicia peered down into the water. A murky green closed in about the hull where the lights shone, and just inches beyond that the light was swallowed by the greasy darkness. She looked up and saw nothing but blackness and felt the damp chill of the atmosphere that closed around them. The complete lack of reference was disorienting.

"It feels like we're moving sideways, but I can't feel any air against me."

"Yes, we're going to back into the area for docking. It makes for an easier exit."

"I feel a little woozy," Alicia said and held her forehead in her left hand as she gripped the lip of the half wall behind which they were standing.

Nemo spoke into his watch. "DOC-medic mode-conn—stat!"

"Affirmative!" came the instantaneous reply. Nemo reached around Alicia and put a hand on each shoulder to steady her. DOC suddenly appeared on the steps below them.

"Take her to sick bay and administer oxygen, provide diagnostic scan. I'll be there momentarily."

"Aye, sir!"

Nemo shifted her to the long arms of the medic and she was whisked down and out of sight. He turned around, grasped a spotlight from the small locker within the compartment, and switching it on, he painted a line at the shore some hundred yards behind the Nautilus. A slight swell and bubbling of water accompanied the ship as she slid backward. Nemo slowly drew the lamp from side to side. Everything looked about the same, no collapsed rock faces or unusual disturbances on the gravel beach. Suddenly the Nautilus stopped moving and Nemo's watch lit up.

"Captain?"

"Yes?"

"We are at the location indicated."

"Very good. Drop all anchors, lower skids, and submerge the vessel at five feet per minute."

"Aye, sir."

Nemo could hear the slight pop of the anchor ports opening as he descended the stairs and the hatch sealed above his head.

Nemo headed for sick bay and was just about to enter when he and Alicia collided. "Whoa! How are you doing?"

"Fine, fine...just short of breath."

Nemo looked past Alicia's shoulder at DOC and raised his eyebrows. "The patient had a mild case of oxygen depletion and lactic acid build-up. After administering oxygen and fluids, her blood oxygen and lactic acid levels are normal."

"Good."

"So, what's happening?" Alicia eagerly inquired.

"Well, right now we're anchored and submerging. The Nautilus will rest on its skids and as the tide rolls out, we'll be able to get to work."

18
DRY DOCK

Alicia begrudgingly put on her dive suit and sat sulking by the dive boot hatch when Nemo entered the chamber and opened a box. "You'll be needing this on shore." Nemo held out what appeared to be a wristwatch, but Alicia suddenly recognized it as the communications interface that Nemo wore on his own wrist and from which he could communicate to the robotic crew. "It's very, very uncomplicated, even easier than a Blackberry or i-Phone," Nemo explained, "no matter what you want to do, just press the button on the upper left corner and speak into the device. It will automatically interpret and execute your orders."

"That's it?"

"That's it. No codes, no stylus, no sequences to remember. You can communicate with me at any time and, of course, with your escort."

"My escort?" Alicia motioned with an uplifted palm.

"I want you to meet another friend of mine," Nemo smirked as he stood aside to let another humanoid enter the chamber. "This is Conseil; he is another version of our steward, but better equipped to navigate various types of terrain. He also has a titanium tote that can hold up to four hundred pounds without upsetting his equilibrium. He is programmed for first aid and protection."

Alicia looked from Nemo to Conseil. Both were about the same height and eerily tilted their heads ever so slightly to the left when not communicating.

"Thanks. I hope he doesn't get in the way."

Conseil's eyes suddenly changed from blue to green. "I'll retain a comfortable distance of your choosing."

Alicia slowly nodded, "Fine. I'm in charge."

"Of course, ma'am."

Alicia couldn't stop the grin from spreading across her face.

Nemo continued his presentation, "Conseil has a full assortment of small excavation tools and programming to identify most known minerals and metals. Just tell him what you need."

"Sounds good," Alicia said enthusiastically, "and what will you be doing?"

"Ulysses, the crew, and Hercules will be carrying out the needed modifications to Nautilus."

"Hercules?"

"Oh, yes, I never mentioned Hercules. He isn't aboard. I left him here on the last visit. Hercules is a construction robot that wasn't one of the casualties at the naval base that exploded. Hercules lacks the character of the others, though he does respond to voice command and can answer in kind. The machine has a number of welding, cutting, and hoisting tools that are needed to execute larger jobs. With appropriate counterweights, it has a one thousand ton lift capacity. So, if you have more than Conseil can manage, give me a call."

At that moment, a chime sounded. "Yes?" Nemo responded, directing his attention to the interface strapped to his wrist.

"The tide is out; depth of remaining water is two feet, three inches," came the report. "Very good. All crew to work detail starting now."

"Aye, sir."

Nemo reached over and with the heel of his hand, struck the large button that signaled the hatch to open. A hiss escaped and as the hatch swept upward, a crew member appeared underneath some eight feet below the bottom. A ladder was quickly connected to the lip of the opening and Nemo proceeded down quickly. Alicia looked out into the murky atmosphere.

"I can barely see a thing," she called down.

"Wait just a second before coming down," Nemo replied. "Activate the quartz lighting system," he ordered to the crew member who had brought the ladder. A moment later the entire area surrounding the Nautilus was illuminated for at least a thousand feet. Alicia could now clearly see her way down and scrambled down the ladder as quickly as the dive suit, so ponderous out of water, would enable her.

"Wow, you didn't say I'd need sunglasses."

"Yes, it's bright at first, but you'll get used to it."

Conseil appeared directly behind Alicia. "Well, your escort is here. Have fun, and remember, he can only handle about four hundred pounds."

"Very funny," Alicia responded, and then turned toward the robot, "keep behind me ten feet, got it?"

"Yes, ma'am."

Nemo watched after them as they made their way down the beach. Every few steps Alicia would stop and stare down at the ground. After a few minutes more, Nemo turned his attention to the matter at hand.

Several crew members brought out an enormous electrical cable and carefully stretched it along the rocky shore and inward next to the rising wall of stone. Had Alicia chosen the opposite direction, she would have rounded the corner of a high outcropping of rock to find herself facing Hercules. The steel and titanium monster sat sleeping like an ancient god, waiting for the right, wakeful incantation. The incantation, in this case, was several million volts of electricity to his lithium batteries. It would take two hours to fully charge those batteries, and afterward, the giant would render several million tons of work before needing another charge.

Meanwhile, inside the Nautilus, other crew were fabricating the necessary modifications to the main ballast tanks. Compartments inside the tanks were taking shape. These bins would hold the exotic quartz that chills salt water on contact. When vented to the outside water, the cold dense water would make sonar detection more difficult, a necessity when navigating populated, warm water seas.

A team of five robots marched down the beach scanning the rock wall that followed it like the cuff of a sleeve. At once, the five converged, and taking position next to one another, began cutting into the rock with laser cutting tools. The bright flicker and smoke gave them the appearance of a single large match being struck by a giant finding his way in the darkness. As they worked, a vehicle resembling an enormous snail with a coil of cable upon its back, no less than twenty feet in height and possessing a large grading blade, made its way toward the five robots and eventually passed them.

The blade in the front of the machine graded the course, rocky earth to a relatively smooth pathway, while a ten ton roller partially concealed in the belly of the machine packed it. Large spindles turned out a continuous line of railroad track that featured a third rail running down the middle. Unlike the outer rails of the track, this center rail featured large teeth, like those on a gear. These teeth would enable a motorized car with a driving cogwheel to gain traction as it pulled its heavy load of quartz back to the Nautilus. Connecting the rails were ties made of high-impact plastic. As the robots worked scanning and excavating the rock face, they traced a vein of the quartz that was deeper and larger than what they could handle. In a few hours, though, a much more capable robot would follow their lead and complete the job in half a day.

19
EXPLORATION

Alicia looked back when the noise of the excavation crew began their work. The sound pealed across the beach and seemed to circle round and up toward the ceiling that must be above, unseen, but held by the simple faith that it just had to be there, holding the weight of the continent. Alicia turned her attention back to the path she was making, the first human perhaps to ever have walked this subterranean earth, this fundamental world. The realization brought a smile to her face and she shook her head in disbelief. Something, though, caught her attention ahead.

A whitish angle protruding from an outcropping of the rock wall brought her running to it. It was a bone! She could not tell what type of bone or how much remained in the rock, but it was something that had been alive at a very early time in the planet's history. She touched the ossified matter and wondered aloud how she could get it out of the rock.

"Ma'am, perhaps I can be of assistance." Conseil's unexpected address startled her.

"Oh, how?"

"Please watch your wrist pad closely for the next few minutes."

With that, Conseil strode to the rock face and extending his arms straight out from his sides, he illuminated a box upon the rock wall. The box fit within the frame created between his arms. The robot bent at the waist toward the ground and then back nearly one hundred degrees and scanned the rock face some twenty-five feet above them. He repeated these actions as he moved down the beach for some fifty feet and then stopped. The box was switched off and his arms rested at his side. He turned toward Alicia and pointed to his wrist and she looked at the LCD of her wrist pad. An image like an X-ray appeared. It was some sort of prehistoric creature, an ichthyosaur of some sort.

"Oh, my God! What is it, what is it!?!"

"Without more precise equipment, it is impossible to say with certainty. From the profile, which is quite good, probably the result of a geologic shearing of the rock face, the fossil does not correspond to any known fossils."

Alicia looked at Conseil from beneath knitted brows. "You're a little windy for a robot."

"I am informative."

"And a character! Say again? There is no known record of this?"

"As far as the data go...no."

Alicia let out a scream that startled Conseil so that he was asking questions about her injury and was moving in to perform first aid.

"No, no, "Alicia, laughed, "I'm fine, really. Just excited."

The robot simply stopped and seemed to stare at her and then shook its head once in affirmation and then negatively from side to side. "I still don't understand this emotion business."

Alicia chuckled and reassured him that he did a wonderful job of scanning. She could have sworn that Conseil stood a little straighter after her compliment.

"How do we get it out?" Alicia eagerly asked.

"Excavation could take considerable time, and I would need additional help from the other crew. I don't know that it is feasible given our time constraints. I will need to check with the Captain."

Alicia pleaded, "Come on, you could do it. Besides, I'm ordering you to do it!"

"Negative. Please check with the Captain," came the abrupt reply.

Alicia now knew the limits of her authority. "Well, Conseil, what do you suggest if we can't excavate this thing?"

"If ma'am would permit me, my scans revealed some matter that, from a preliminary scan, seemed to indicate the possibility, a possibility of 65.7%, of the presence of..."

"Spit it out!"

"Diamonds."

"Diamonds!?!" exclaimed Alicia.

20

A GIRL'S BEST FRIEND

It was a cliché, of course, but for that it was no less true. Nemo had programmed Conseil to suggest what might be most appealing for Alicia. And what woman, no matter how fiercely independent, professional, and objective doesn't like diamonds? Given any other reference point, Alicia would have chaffed at such an obvious appeal to stereotyping, but diamonds have a magical effect on women.

"Hurry up! Hurry up! Start digging!" she ordered.

If the machine could have smirked, it would have, but instead only complied with a loud "Yes, ma'am!" Moving with precision and dexterity, the robot again framed a glowing box on an area of shoreline that butted against the rock face.

"Step back and shield your eyes. Do not look at the cutting lasers until I signal that it is safe."

"Give me a break," Alicia countered, "now I can't watch you excavate the greatest treasures in the world!?!"

"I shall not proceed unless you comply with the safety regulations prescribed for a non-emergency event."

With that, Conseil plopped down before Alicia, sitting Indian-style on spindly legs.

"You're pulling a Mahatma Gandhi on me!?!" Alicia incredulously shouted. There was no response. Once again, Alicia was met with a futile situation, though her life wasn't at stake so much as was a possible supplement to her income.

"Fine. Do your thing. I'll even turn my back so as not to peek. Is that satisfactory?"

"Completely, ma'am."

"Yeah, yeah," Alicia grumbled.

Picking up where he left off, Conseil moved closer to the site and bending precisely at the waist, he held his arms forward and two barrels, similar to those which equipped Ulysses, unfolded and locked into place. After a pause of half a second, red beams traced an unseen template registered in his central processing unit. Smoke at first wisped from the cutting points, but then began to thicken and then billow from the deepening incision. After precisely two minutes, the lasers switched off. Smoke still bled from the wounded rock face. "It is safe to look," Conseil called to Alicia. She turned and ran to the area, anticipating some sort of heap of diamonds spilled like so many coins from a winning slot machine.

"Well?"

"I need to shift the sediment to extract the diamonds. Please, step to the side and I'll begin."

Alicia obediently did so and, as she did, the robot's hands folded underneath his forearms, and two scoop-like trowels with sharpened steel teeth folded out from the top of the forearms. Locking into place with a click, the robot moved in to scoop out the earth.

"What is the composition of the rock? " Alicia asked.

"It is an unusually rich mixture of quartzes, corundum, granite, and diamond. I can continue this process for only another five minutes before my tools need resurfacing."

With power typical of much heavier equipment, Conseil split, scooped, and removed rock so dense and hard that typical small construction equipment would have been stalled. Still, fired by her desire for the icy treasure beneath the surface, Alicia suggested additional equipment be fetched from the Nautilus. "Would a...a Bobcat help the process along?"

"A Bobcat, which the Nautilus does not possess, is only half as powerful as my arms are when my body is properly braced."

"Oh." Alicia's curiosity was piqued, "Are you the most powerful of the crew?" Alicia asked.

"No. The most powerful crew member is Hercules with a one thousand ton capacity. Ulysses can lift a hundred tons. The stewards are somewhat less. Though outfitted differently, I am identical in specification to the stewards."

"What of DOC?"

"DOC's specifications are known only to the Captain."

"Of course," she concluded.

A shrill buzzing startled Alicia and she jumped back and looked out toward the black waters, "What is it? What's wrong?"

"That is the ten minute tide warning. I shall scoop what we have cleared and bring it back to Nautilus for processing. This won't take but two minutes and forty five seconds."

Without waiting for a response, the robot bent sharply on its knees and then turned its head around to view behind it. One arm dismantled the pick that was in place and restored the titanium hand that typically served the arm. Leaning back, Conseil scooped with the other hand that was still outfitted with a shovel. True to his word, nearly four hundred pounds of silt had been collected and sealed in under three minutes. "We need to return to Nautilus," Conseil concluded as he stood up and pivoted his head back to its normal position.

"Fine with me," Alicia responded, "I am hungry and a little tired. Odd. I wasn't tired just a little while ago. I'm getting a headache, too."

She began to move forward when Conseil gently put a hand on her arm, "Stop, ma'am. Do not exert yourself. You may be suffering from hypoxia. Allow me." Conseil scooped Alicia in his arms.

"Hey, what the...," Alicia stammered. She was being shifted and cradled by Conseil. With the same bounding motions that Alicia had first experienced when the steward had carried her onto the deck of the Nautilus, Conseil was transporting her back to the ship. She never finished her sentence. The sensation of speed along with his vaulting over small obstacles and the pounding of her head made speech impossible. It was, though, unneeded.

Conseil had electronically transmitted this information to Nemo as well as DOC. Alicia barely saw the ascent up the ladder and the sprint down the long corridor to the sickbay. Gently, almost tenderly, Conseil laid her down on the bed and stepped back without taking his eyes off her. DOC began to administer oxygen and to remove her diving suit. As soon as the linked shells of armor were off, he began diagnostic tests. Nemo appeared at the door and Alicia noticed him from above her oxygen mask. "What's happening?"

"Don't talk, just breathe. You might have a bit of hypoxia. You're low on oxygen and you need to recover. Just rest."

Alicia thought she had never heard a finer suggestion in her life and drowsed off.

After a few moments when she had entered a deeper state of sleep, Nemo moved toward the bed.

"Sir, the patient is suffering from hypoxia. With oxygen and hydration, she should make a full recovery. The reduced level of oxygen and the difference of barometric pressure in this environment will aggravate her condition. I suggest pressurizing her room if departure to more normal atmospheric conditions does not occur within the next 48 hours."

"Thank you, DOC. We should be leaving this place before then."

Nemo reached down and felt the cool skin of Alicia's arm and he pulled a blanket up and gently draped it around her shoulders. Though in deep sleep, she responded to the added warmth and her knitted brows relaxed.

21
ETIQUETTE OF SORROW

Nemo was starting his second plate of Ahi tuna and what tasted like a caper sauce when Alicia entered the salon. Her hair was clipped in back and she wore sweats and slippers. "Hello. How are you feeling?"

"Not well. I still don't have any energy and I feel achy everywhere. I am hungry, though, and DOC suggested eating as much as I could handle, something about 'extra caloric consumption in these atmospheric conditions.'"

Nemo said nothing for a few moments as he considered this recommendation. "Yes, that makes perfect sense. DOC's fuzzy logic processing unit is paying off."

"What are you talking about?" Alicia asked irritably as she took her place at the table. "Some years ago IBM had created a computer called Big Blue that was able to beat a chess champion. The computer was able to make choices based upon data. DOC is deducing and making recommendations; that's all. Have a roll."

"I could really go for a cigarette."

"No, I wouldn't. Your system is already starved for oxygen. Drink plenty of water and eat."

"So what's happening to me?"

"The atmospheric conditions here are similar to what they would be in a high altitude environment. Your body is reacting and trying to compensate for what is probably a significantly lower oxygen level." Nemo paused, looked down at his plate and then raised his eyes, "You know, I never bothered checking it. When I found this caldera, I was so excited I just went to work without bothering with tests."

"So why aren't you in this miserable condition?"

"Don't know. Maybe I was a Sherpa in a former life."

As Alicia ate and drank she felt energy return and every ten minutes her headache subsided. "How long are we going to be here?"

"Well, the mining is going very well and the crew are nearly finished with the modifications to the ballast tanks. I need to work on the finer parts of the mechanism of activation and flow. We should be out of here within forty-eight hours, though."

"Oh," Alicia flatly commented.

"Why, you seem disappointed?"

"Well, we started a conversation about some things that I'd like to pursue, to have some clarity on."

"Go ahead," Nemo encouraged her.

"I don't want to rush it and I don't want to hold back our progress. I don't like feeling like this and..." Nemo raised one finger of the hand that was cupping his water goblet.

"Please, don't worry about that. You'll be in no danger. We're going to pressurize some portion of Nautilus so that the barometric pressure will be the same as at sea level. So please, we have all the time we need."

"All the time we need?"

"Sorry?"

"You just said, 'all the time we need'."

"Yes, for our conversation," confirmed Nemo.

"Right. Don't mind me. Yes, remember when we were discussing your situation and whether those who were attacking you were justified?"

Nemo inhaled deeply and quickly so that it was audible as the air passed through his nostrils.

"Yes?"

"Well, why don't you think it just that people are attacking you? Haven't you attacked and killed?"

This was a conversation Nemo had hoped to avoid, though he knew that avoidance was impossible with Alicia. He knew his response, though. He had had this conversation long before Alicia came aboard, long before Nautilus slipped away from its pen and dove so deep and so far away from the terrible concussion of the blast. "I was to develop technology to destroy those who would jeopardize our American way of life. I have no remorse for that; I embraced that job not only as a patriotic duty, but as a personal duty. It was, if you pardon the cliché, a labor of love, truly." Nemo paused and bit the corner of his lower lip. "The agreement was that they would protect my family from the enemy. A simple social contract, an easy quid pro quo—and perhaps a naïve faith on my part. They butchered my family, Al Qaeda, the Navy, the NCIS."

"What are you saying? The Navy didn't do anything to harm your family, they—"

"You are such a child!" Nemo savagely interrupted and sprang up, knocking his chair over backward. "One simple assignment, to protect one family of three adults and two children and they didn't do it. They did not! It was not for lack of ability or failure in action taken, it was a failure of the will. They would not do what they could have done so easily."

He was breathing heavy and stepped back to restore his chair. Alicia sat stunned with her mouth open. Nemo plopped down heavily into the chair and let his legs sprawl from beyond the width of the seat. He did not look at her. Tears flowed freely over his puffy eyelids and dampened his shirt collar.

She asked for it and she had gotten it. She couldn't think, but only feel. She rose and moved toward where he sat, crumpled, his head down in dejection. She would not intrude upon his grief; she would return to her own room, but as she passed him she stopped and slowly, almost imperceptibly, bent down and placed a kiss, light yet firm, just above his left ear. She straightened up and moved forward in one motion and had left the room before he realized what had happened.

Once back outside her room, she found Conseil posted outside her door. "What's this about?"

"I'll be your steward, ma'am."

"What of the usual steward?"

Conseil didn't answer at first, but then blurted, "He's been assigned elsewhere."

"I see."

"Ma'am?" Conseil added.

"Yes?"

"I am to assist you in any way. Your cabin has been pressurized to sea level, and consequently there is more resistance when opening the door. The Captain has ordered me to perform tasks that may at this time be fatiguing for you."

"Oh, I appreciate that. But I'm feeling up to opening my own door," and with that Alicia grasped the handle and gave a good yank that succeeded in doing nothing but sealing the door even tighter. Another attempt with her weight against it did even less.

"Really, ma'am!" Conseil shook his head in disapproval and reached out and pulled the door open as though it were the lightest screen door. Alicia wondered why she kept underestimating these mechanical crew members and why she kept overestimating her ability to force her will on a world determined by physics and steel.

"Thank you, Conseil; that'll be all. I'm going to rest and you can stay outside the door." "Yes, ma'am. Would you care for anything from the galley?"

"No, I'm fine."

"Good evening, then."

"Good evening, Conseil."

Once sealed in, Alicia reflected on what a character the robot was. It almost had a personality. "Fuzzy logic run amuck," she told herself. If the robots were seeming more human, Nemo was seeming less of a robot. Alicia reflected on his earlier polarity of kind etiquette and cold killing. But it wasn't cold; no, it was hot with emotion, flickering with hate and love, and guilt. Alicia knew Nemo felt no guilt over those he drowned, but searing remorse over those he did not protect within his own home. He was a raw wound and would never heal.

Alicia looked down at the pendulous watch that had slid back over the lower portion of her forearm. Did she feel that she didn't do enough to save her brother? Perhaps, but he was a grown man and bore responsibility for his actions. Still, Alicia knew she wasn't satisfied with that tidy summation. She thought of the Nautilus attacking the drug boats. Did she gasp at the initial carnage of agony and hopeless clawing toward the air? "Of course," she assured herself. It was horrifying, and turned her stomach. She regretted her agreement to that. Most importantly, did she feel guilt over those drug dealers whose bones had since been picked clean? The answer came back to her conscience, quick and clean. The sobering reality was that she felt no remorse at all. With a single sweeping motion, the watch was removed and placed upon the dressing table.

Alicia walked over to her bed and pulled off her sweatshirt and, bending forward, stripped off her sweatpants. The coolness felt good against her flushed skin. She lay down atop the bed. She wondered if those philosophers had been right: was Nemo, surviving here at the bottom of the ocean, at the bottom of the world, out of reach of time itself; was Nemo beyond good and evil? Was she, too, or was she just along for the ride? Despite the fact that her room was pressurized, her head began to pound and she tightly shut her eyes. Within a few minutes her creased forehead relaxed and a light snoring emitted from between her slightly parted lips.

22
WAKING NIGHTMARE

Alicia awoke with a start. Beads of perspiration were sprouting from the pores of her scalp and she felt clammy everywhere. She looked about her room and everything was as it had been. Yet, something was not right; she could feel it. She swung her legs over the side of her bed and stood, pausing, listening. Nothing was to be heard. She grabbed her sweatpants and quickly wiped the cool sweat that had settled over her skin like a sick dew. She put on her pants and sweatshirt, slipped into her felt boots and quickly walked to the door. Remembering the pressurization, she called out to Conseil on the other side. The door instantly opened and Conseil inquired about her health. For no apparent reason she was worried, "Where's Nemo?"

"The Captain is topside taking observations on the conning tower."

Alicia pushed past the robot and ran aft toward the connecting staircase to the hatch.

Making her way to the top, she exited and saw Nemo far down past the forecastle, standing at the edge where the hull sloped into the water. Alicia was struggling for breath and panting, but was relieved to see that he wasn't alone; DOC stood sentry-like next to him. After the sound of the blood thumping in her own ears subsided, she could hear Nemo's voice weakly speaking. The strange acoustics of the caldera brought the sounds to her as though he were standing next to her.

"Why?... What should I do?... It is hopeless...," and then a chain of twisted sobs broke out. Having caught her breath, Alicia jogged down the deck to where he stood. DOC stood, passive and mute, not realizing what was taking place. How could he? Even the superlative logic of his central processor could not deduce emotion, let alone guilt and regret. Alicia reached up and put her left arm around Nemo's shoulder. He stood staring at the water and so she focused on where he was looking.

There in the greasy black of the water, just beyond the underwater lights, black shapes, large and thick, writhed in liquid shadow. They stayed just beyond the distinguishing reach of the lights, but were still discernible. "I ruined everything," Nemo said in an exhausted wisp of breath. Alicia knew better than to try to soothe him by saying that he was wrong about all that occurred and all that he had been living with for so long.

"You were in a tough position. You made choices, some of them wrong, some of them completely justified."

"Yes. The worst decision killed them all. The just decision was to leave with what little I had left. But I killed them!"

Nemo's renewed vigor alarmed Alicia. What was he going to do, jump off into the murky depths and end it all? The roiling beneath the liquid film began to break the surface.

"Nemo, get away from it!" Alicia shouted. He remained implacable. "Nemo!" she pleaded. DOC suddenly shifted to combat mode; the arms raised and precisely leveled at the center of the shapes beneath the surface. A weapon of some sort unfolded from each forearm and locked into place. Alicia grasped Nemo's arms and turned him to face her.

"Nemo, come on! I have to get back home. I have to get back home. Don't take me with you; I don't want to die like this down here!"

His reverie was broken. "Okay. Yes. Of course. You've mentioned home before." Like a sleepwalker, Nemo slowly faced his intended direction and made his way to the conning tower. Alicia shifted her eyes toward the water, but all was calm, the usual dark murk, nothing more. She then ran back toward where Nemo had begun walking. Moments after she had left, DOC disengaged and made his way back to his post atop the same tower.

23
PRODUCTIVITY

Alicia couldn't believe what she was witnessing. Nemo had preceded her by only moments, but already the relaxed, easygoing pace of work that had characterized the berth in this port had instantly been replaced by frenetic activity. Robots she hadn't known were on board were now everywhere. Some were very sleek machines, painted and outlined in LEDs. Others were obviously hastily constructed, with no coverings to conceal moving parts, and sometimes, missing an appendage. Still they worked. They passed each other torches and tools. Others crawled about like enormous spiders, but instead of spinning webs, they laid electrical cable and wound wires around now exposed piping and through open panels. It was as though Nemo had willed this instantaneous work. Robots were everywhere and the noise was becoming deafening. Nemo was nowhere to be found, though.

She tried to ask some of these machines where Nemo was, but they only paused and then returned to their labors. She went to his cabin but found it empty, along with the salon, the gallery, and, her last hope, the conn. Frustrated and worried, she yelled at the top of her lungs, "Conseil!" The walls, thick with monitors, control panels and wiring, mocked her shout with silence. Alicia let her head drop. Exhaustion was again weighing upon her. Her head began to pound and she swung out one of the attached stools that folded into the large map table in the center of the room. As she perched heavily upon the seat, a green light switched on over her head and Conseil's voice sounded through the room.

"Ma'am? I'm so sorry, but the Captain needed all hands and he especially needed my expertise in situational analytics to address potential problems with the modifications being made to the new stealth system."

"Conseil!"

"Ma'am!"

"Is he all right?"

"Yes, ma'am. Perfectly fine. He asks that you return to your room for rest; the door has been left open and the room will pressurize as soon as the door is shut. Do you need assistance?"

"No. I think I'll take his advice. I can make my way back there."

The walk back to her room seemed to take forever, especially since she had to move carefully around uprooted piping, cables sprouting out from the walls, and robots with unfinished, sharp steel edges moving about with superhuman reflexes and strength. As she found her corridor, her body began to ache for rest. She welcomed the slicing of air as the door sealed her in and shut out all that noise. She pulled off her clothes and let them lay where they fell and slid into bed. The crisp sheets poured around her body in delicious coolness and then her body grew limp with the increasing warmth of the blanket insulating her own body heat. A contented sigh came from under the covers, and she was fully and happily asleep.

Three stories beneath Alicia, Nemo stood in a tee shirt and pants made with a heavy material with thick, leather reinforced patches on the knees. His shirt was dripping with perspiration and grease was smeared on his forehead, face, and chest. Even Conseil had grease pasted on his hands and forearms. Both watched as a ball-cock valve some six feet in diameter opened and closed as Nemo would call out an order. "Cold water infusion, open! Cold water infusion, close!"

"It appears to be working, sir."

"Yes. Conseil, program a few other variations like 'cold inject' and 'CWI' for voice activation."

"Yes, sir."

"What's the status of the ballast modification?"

"Sir, the ballast tanks themselves are complete, but a simulation showed that there was excessive noise as the water flowed into the quartz chambers. To mitigate this problem, I ordered the ballast tanks to be coated with T-11 insulating material. It not only reduces noise as a buffer, but reduces undue friction on its surface."

"Excellent. Run simulations as soon as the coating has cured and report back to me. Also, go back to that dig site you and Alicia were at and take a crew with you. Get as much as you can that will be portable for her."

"Yes, Captain."

"Oh, and how much power reserve do we have?"

"Yes. I was going to discuss this with you, sir."

"Well?" Nemo prodded the eccentric machine.

"We are down to our last six hours."

"How much energy does the crew have?"

"On average, each member has approximately two hours left. It will take four hours of work to put everything back together."

"We're done with Hercules?"

"Yes. Hercules is parked and has been switched to stand-by."

"How much power does he have left?" Nemo asked, making some calculations of his own.

"One moment, sir. Let me access that line. Just now sir, Hercules contains one megawatt of electricity."

"What can we accomplish with that megawatt? I really hate to run this silty water from the caldera through the turbines."

"One megawatt would enable us to fully charge the crew and would give the Nautilus one-quarter propulsion for one hour."

"Very good. Reverse charge and refresh the crew in shifts. Prioritize propulsive and stealth features. When able, get back to shore and finish that mining."

"Aye, Captain," returned Conseil.

24

UNDERWAY AND UNDERSTOOD

Alicia awoke slowly and dozed intermittently for about an hour. Her body felt heavy, but rested, comfortable. Her skin was warm but dry, with no sensation of having been chilled. She stared at the ceiling and noticed for the first time the arabesques of the frosted light fixtures. She turned on her side and yawned. She was suddenly aware of her desire for a shower, hot and steamy with a cleansing, high-pressure rinse. She sat up and swung her legs out of bed and made her way to the toilet and shower area.

Delightful was the word as she basked in the warmth and patter of the water. The soaps and lotions aboard were unmistakably masculine, but were nonetheless clean and refreshing in aroma. Alicia did not mind at all. In fact, she liked the idea that this man's sense of personal comfort and preference was made known to her. Previously, it made Nemo a little more human to her, tenuous and uncertain as that seemed before. Now, though, it was a different story. No tell-tale signs of his humanity were now needed. He was more than a scarred man. He was an open wound, raw and dangerous.

Unlike with other men, this was not a weakness in her eyes. Nemo did not whine or mope about. He was often morose, it is true, and the events at the caldera were more than frightening; they were positively dreadful—yes, that was the term she introduced to Nemo before she had even witnessed the sickening display of dark motion in the murk. Alicia turned the shower a little hotter and increased the pressure of the spray to dispel the picture from her recollection. She continued with her disquisition. Nemo, above all, was a man of action. His study of the ocean, his engineering and exploration, even his plundering of others' champagne— she smiled at this thought— these aspects made Nemo unique from others who might have lain about and wallowed in self-pity.

Alicia had turned off the water and as she did so she heard knocking at her door. "Yes?" she called.

"Ma'am," Conseil responded, "the Captain requests that you join him in the conn. We are about to make passage out of the caldera. It is a safety measure."

Alicia was taken aback by the sudden completion of the work that had been going on. "I'll be there in five minutes."

"Very good. You should have no problem opening the door; the entire ship has been pressurized."

Alicia hastily dried herself and picked out clean clothes from the wardrobe. She chose lightweight navy pants and a crimson tee-shirt that featured the golden nautilus motif over the left breast. She slipped on the soft chukka boots and, running a comb through her still damp hair, made her way aft to the conn.

As she climbed toward the entrance to the conn, she noticed how much more energy she had and she realized that her headache was completely gone. She didn't see Nemo as she made the top of the stairway, but DOC was standing at attention to the left of the opening. Nemo turned as he anticipated her entry. Both spoke at the same moment and Nemo chuckled. "How did you sleep?"

"I slept well, but you didn't sleep at all."

"No, I wanted to get done and get out."

"Nemo, what were those things in the water, that darkness in the shadows?"

Nemo's face turned a grayish pallor. "I don't know. I have recorded and analyzed the phenomena as much as I am able. I don't know... 'more things in heaven and earth than are dreamt of in my philosophy.' But I do know that you saved my life back there and I thank you." Nemo stepped forward and in one movement put his arms around Alicia, embracing her strongly and tenderly. She hardly knew what was happening and it ended. Nemo stepped back, smiling, looking into her eyes and then turning away to oversee the control panel. She remained, fixed in the same position. Her mind was numb at first and then, as any woman would, she put the emotional pieces into place, quickly and accurately. She no longer feared for her safety or worried about Nemo's sanity. She no longer cared about whether Nemo thought he was justified or self-deluded.

"We'll be sealing all compartments momentarily. Is there anything you need?"

Without hesitation, Alicia responded, "I'd like a cold glass of water."

"Of course. Bring a carafe of water and tumblers, Conseil."

Alicia hadn't even noticed the robot now standing opposite of DOC. With a simple "Sir!", Conseil acknowledged Nemo's order. In less than a minute, the robot was carefully pouring the clear, cold liquid and without ceremony, Alicia guzzled down one full glass and then another. "Oh, my!" uttered Conseil, and Nemo broke out laughing.

25
RECHARGING

Alicia noticed all the red lights on the control panel, lights that had been previously green. "Is that a problem?" she asked, nodding toward the walls.

"It could be. We are very low on power. I could open the vents and use the water propulsion system, but the silty water of the caldera is not the best thing for the machinery. We have been working on battery and doing a lot of work with that power. Once we move into the ocean proper, we can open the vents and move out and charge the batteries. We'll be in an area that is very difficult for anyone to detect us. It's deeper than military submarines can dive and the ocean floor and currents make echo location more difficult. Besides, no one in the area would use active sonar, bouncing pings all over the place. Once a boat pings, its position is no longer hidden. Besides, the modified ballast system should provide an extra degree of camouflage, so to speak."

Nemo continued, thinking aloud, "Getting back to the battery situation, I'm not comfortable sailing for any place with no battery reserve. We'll stay put and charge the system at least half way before moving on."

"Where are we headed?"

"Well, Alicia, I promised to get you home. Any trail that the Navy might have been following has long since disappeared. A port friendly to Americans that provides a ready means of return to the U.S., while not compromising my security, is where we need to go."

"Oh, right," Alicia responded flatly.

"Unless, of course, you had some other destination in mind," Nemo offered, smiling. He was gauging her reaction and now she knew it. She arched her eyebrows and then her eyes narrowed to feline slits. Her anger was a bluff and Nemo knew it.

"You are a devious man," she concluded.

"Yes, and you act surprised every time!"

Alicia shook her head and grinned in spite of herself.

"Really, though, Alicia, it is perfectly safe for you to make your way back. You'll have money, false identification, anything you would need to get back home without running afoul of the port authorities. If refugees south of Texas can get into the U.S.

and work and live under the government's nose, you better believe I can get you back in."

"No, it's not that," she responded, "there is just so much more of this world that I want to experience."

"You mean the mad escape from the U.S. Navy and the slimy, toxic atmosphere of the cave weren't enough?"

Alicia smiled and quickly added, "Come on, you promised giant squid and now you aren't going to deliver? What of other treasure? Didn't you need more champagne? Don't you need to replenish your supplies? This is all so fascinating!"

"Ah, yes, the squid. And you have, in fact, been eating everything not bolted down. Are there any particular wrecks that you would visit?"

"The Titanic!"

Nemo whistled through his teeth and held up his hands, waving off the suggestion. "You don't fool around, do you? No, that's too risky."

"Too risky?"

"Yes, it's like Disneyland right now. There are subs with tourists, scientific expeditions, treasure hunters like yourself..." Alicia tsked him and made a face, "...and you better believe there is some military or Coast Guard surveillance as well. With all that traffic and activity, somebody is going to get into trouble and will need to be rescued. Those are dangerous waters, in any case."

Alicia wasn't about to give up, though. "You just told me that you can get me back into the U.S. without a problem. Now you're telling me that a shipwreck 12,000 feet at the bottom of the North Atlantic is impossible because there may be a few tourists in the area in fragile little submarines with little round windows no bigger than a dinner plate?"

Nemo grinned but then, intrigued by Alicia's enthusiasm, he asked Alicia to explain herself. "Well, what would you want to see, Alicia?"

"What do you mean?"

"Put another way," explained Nemo, "what do you think you're going to find there?"

Alicia could tell that he was about to take exception to exploring the Titanic, but rather than engage in debate, she waited for him to explain himself. Cleverly, she shook her head and shrugged her shoulders in response to his query.

A few seconds later, her strategy was proven as Nemo began his argument. "The Titanic has been exploited to such a degree that the enormity of what occurred is lost on people. People have this ghoulish fascination to see shoes on the bottom of the ocean and witness remnants of an elegant party at the same time. There is nothing elegant about what happened. Also, the accepted story of how the ship sank is incorrect. A three hundred foot gash would have sunk the liner in a matter of minutes; it would never have stayed afloat for as long as it did. They run computer models but never an actual model. Computer models are limited by their programmers. I never entirely trust computer models. In fact, as we're recharging, I'm going to take the Nautilus' exploratory shuttle and assess just how effective our modifications are."

Alicia was intrigued by what she had just heard. "Well, do you know how it sank?"

Needing no other encouragement, Nemo, the scholar, launched into a detailed lecture on the well-worn topic of how the Titanic really sank. "The best theory ever offered," he began, "was from Edward Wilding, an architect from the company of Harland and Wolff, the firm that built the Titanic."

"After the great ship went down," he explained, "there were investigations, of course, both in England and America. Wilding testified at some of those hearings. From descriptions of survivors and with what had been known of the pattern of flooding, he surmised that several smaller sections in a few compartments were responsible. Although this seemed to have been confirmed by a well publicized expedition in 1996 using advanced side sonar equipment, there is more to the story.

Like Wilding, there have been other more recent proponents of the "grounding" theory."

Alicia furrowed her brow and raised her hand slightly to give pause.

"Right," acknowledged Nemo, "simply put, grounding theories maintain the notion that the ship didn't simply scrape the side of an iceberg, but actually ran up on a section of it. Both Wilding, who had brilliantly deduced the process of the destruction, and the more recent grounding theorists are correct. However, Wilding's estimation and even the damage confirmed by the '96 analysis don't account for the rapid and inevitable flooding that occurred. "

Ordinarily, Alicia either laughed or yawned at discussions of this sort and the melodrama of investigators hashing out details in the fashion of cable television shows claiming to be 'investigative'. This, however, was very much real and she suspected that this particular investigator speaking had much more to offer.

Nemo continued his analysis, building toward what promised to be a unique solution. "Side sonar is limited in that it isn't an X-ray; it does not go beyond the parameters of the hull into the interior," Nemo explained. He paused, and with a smile spreading across his face, he triumphantly explained his conclusion. "Within the forward compartments, coming through the double hull on both sides of the keel are two holes. One is approximately eight feet long and approximately three feet wide and the other is smaller; about four feet long and about a foot and a half wide. Given these penetrations, coupled with sheared rivets and buckled plating on the starboard side, the rapid flooding is understood.

The impact just didn't punch two neat holes, either," Nemo added. "The Titanic, nearly fifty thousand tons, struck the iceberg at over twenty knots. That's a hell of a lot of force! The berg was large and the ship did, by everyone's account, scrape along it. The force punctured the double hull and weakened some forward bulkheads in the process. That, along with the force of the gushing water, rendered a couple of the bulkheads ineffective at containing the flooding. You know the rest of the story."

Alicia followed his logic, but it could not be verified simply from an exercise of deduction. "How do you know this?" Alicia asked directly.

"I've been there," Nemo responded. "Ulysses and I made our way in and down. It's as obvious as can be. One can see the damage. The decking is puckered and burst through as though enormous bullets were fired through the bottom of the vessel. It's awful. And you better believe there are human remains in those areas—it's ghastly. I have no trophies from that wreck."

"My God! All the researchers have said that the lower levels are inaccessible."

"Yes, inaccessible to them. They have unmanned vehicles on little tethers and myopic viewfinders. Please!" Nemo dismissed the researchers with a wave of his hand and he looked away in disgust. Thinking that exploration of the Titanic was now a closed topic, Alicia was surprised by Nemo's reconsideration of her request.

"Still, I understand your curiosity," Nemo rejoined, "and, after all, I had been there myself, right? We'll go and see what we can. Keep in mind that the structure is being eaten away by iron consuming bacteria-the rusticles you see in all the photos- and much of the wreck is unstable. The sections I had explored may very well be collapsed and out of reach. There are limits to what Ulysses can do. The Titanic is," paused Nemo, "well, it is titanic! Hercules would be needed for major excavation," he concluded.

"Thank you, I appreciate that very much," Alicia responded, genuinely enthused. "Was the Titanic poorly constructed with inferior steel as everyone claims?"

"Heavens, no! Take this from someone who does this for a living: Harland and Wolff did a magnificent job with the Titanic. People look back and nitpick, 'the rivets were lousy; the steel was brittle,' and then, on a more poetic note, they claim that the designers' hubris sunk the liner. Ridiculous!"

Alicia hadn't expected so much passion on this topic; she wouldn't have dared to change the subject, though, especially since she had mentioned it first.

"Not too long ago," Nemo added, "a cruise ship was steaming along the coast of Antarctica and struck ice and sunk. Fortunately, a distress call was made early and everyone was rescued. This was a modern vessel with watertight bulkheads through-out. Is anyone claiming that the steel prematurely gave way? I'll never forget the period just after 9/11. Everyone was dismayed that the Towers fell so soon after being struck. One architect had the presence of mind to set the media right. It was a marvel, he said, that the Towers remained standing as long as they did. So, given the fact that no one has satisfactorily determined the size, shape, and density of ice of the berg that Titanic struck, I'd say that the 'experts' are blowing smoke. I wonder if they realize this or are as ignorant as they are arrogant."

At that moment a gong lightly sounded. "Ah, we're just passing the mouth of the vent—and not a moment too soon." Another row of red lights came on and a monitor flashed on with numbers and a graph showing how much power was still available. Ventilation, heat and water were sustainable for only another four hours. "Wow! We ran it close." exclaimed Nemo. "The venturis will need to be opened by air pressure." Nemo walked over to a computer console and typed for about ten seconds. "We'll need to wait a few minutes until our stationary thrusters can be operated. The propulsion doesn't have a neutral, so to speak. It relies on a series of moveable thrusters."

Alicia turned toward the sound as the outer doors were slid open and the room perceptibly lurched forward. Tens of thousands of gallons now flowed through the turbines every minute. After only a few minutes, rows of red lights were turning green. Nemo typed at the console and then paused, looking up at the one monitor that depicted a graph. Satisfied with what he saw, he stood up from the console. "She'll charge at 70% while 30% will be directed to propulsion and needed systems. Once we're finished with tests of the new sonar baffle system, we'll be on our way."

"To the Titanic!" exclaimed Alicia.

"No," Nemo cut her off, "at least not directly. You're a high maintenance woman and consume only the finest food and champagne. We need to do some fishing and some shopping." Alicia ignored his comment. "Where, then?"

"I don't know. I was thinking the Sea of Japan. We can fill our freezers and see giant squid."

Alicia smiled warmly and resisted the urge to hug Nemo. She was thrilled to be seeing some of the most amazing sights and be witness to one of the most prominent historical events in the popular imagination. She pictured herself among the strewn artifacts of the Titanic, wishing she could capture the moment forever. She remembered Nemo's disapproval with those who have exploited the Titanic. Her face dropped, but not without being noticed.

"What's wrong?" Nemo asked about her sudden, apparent dismay.

"Oh, I just would have liked to have taken something with me from the Titanic, as a memento."

"Of course."

"You mean you don't mind? I thought you just said that…"

"Yes, yes. I was talking about those who run tourism businesses off the tragedy and sell artifacts. My sense is that you won't be selling anything to the highest bidder."

"Well no, of course not," Alicia assured him, "it would be for me and me alone. The remembrance of our, I mean my time," she corrected herself, "at the site." She looked Nemo in the eye and tried to determine whether he caught her slip up. If he did, he showed no sign.

"No problem, Alicia. Now, how about something to eat and then we'll get to work? You can come along in the shuttle if you like." Alicia nodded eagerly and Nemo gave the appropriate orders to Conseil who then managed the steward and the other machines.

Lunch wasn't nearly as sumptuous as previous meals had been, just some chowder and a few simply prepared fillets of snapper. "As you can see, Alicia, the larder is almost empty."

"You know, I rather like this simple meal, though," and as she said so she turned to the plates before her with gusto.

"So, tell me about this shuttle."

"Well, the Nautilus was originally conceived as a multi-purpose vessel which included the ability to operate missions employing Special Forces like SEAL teams. A submersible was designed that could move quickly, maneuver sharply, dive deeply and also hold personnel and equipment. The shuttle never was given a name, but I call it the Cousteau."

"As in Jacques Cousteau?"

"Yes, I loved watching his television programs when I was a kid and I always wanted to be like him, exploring the oceans and seeing the wonders of the watery inner world of our planet."

"So, no weapons aboard?" questioned Alicia.

"The Cousteau? Not a single weapon. It is now for reconnaissance of a peaceful nature. True, it has the latest in sonar equipment which we'll be using to test Nautilus' new systems, but it is now equipped with research tools."

"I see," Alicia replied, "and what of the Nautilus? Does it have any weapons?" Nemo hadn't expected this question, but understood its relevance given the context and purpose for what the ship was originally designed. "Nautilus has mostly defensive, that is to say, evasive type equipment. There are no ballistic missiles aboard and the usual assortment of torpedoes isn't present. Nautilus has a few experimental torpedoes aboard, but they themselves wouldn't inflict much damage on any battle group. Once detected, the Nautilus is as vulnerable as a World War II U-Boot would be."

Alicia wasn't convinced, "Come on, you mean to tell me that this sub possesses no advantage?"

"Relative to other submarines, yes. It dives deeper, maneuvers better, and goes much faster. You must understand, though, that the U.S. Navy as well as American allies have the Barracuda."

"Barracuda," Alicia interrupted, "that name rings a bell. Isn't that some sort of super fast torpedo?"

"Oh, yes! It is rocket propelled and travels at over three hundred and fifty knots. It's essentially the underwater equivalent of a bullet. Once you're spotted, you're dead; it's just a matter of seconds before it occurs."

"There's no way to counteract it or throw it off course?"

"I wouldn't say 'no way', but it's difficult and I'm not in that line of work anymore. The bottom line is that enough conventional torpedoes will do the job if they are used intelligently. The Nautilus works in the same medium and is subject to all the laws of physics that submariners have faced since the very beginning. It's a more slippery fish, to be sure, but is a fish, nonetheless. It takes a wider net to catch it, but it still only takes a net."

"You seem pretty resigned to this fatal perspective. Why, then, all these modifications?"

"Alicia, I'm not ready to die yet. There is more for me in the ocean to occupy my mind, engage my spirit."

Alicia believed him and quickly finished off her lunch.

26

SEA TRIALS

After lunch, Alicia followed Nemo way aft to the stern of Nautilus. "Wow, how long is this boat?"

"The Nautilus is an even 600 feet in length, larger than the Soviet Typhoon. She is 60 feet in beam or width and she draws thirty-two feet of water. I'm sure you noticed how low she sits on the surface."

Alicia's mouth dropped open. "This thing is a monster!"

"Yes, I probably should have christened it Leviathan, but the uniforms were already made," Nemo joked.

As they neared the rear, Alicia noticed how the walls gradually turned inward and the passage narrowed. "Okay, we're going to make our way up a small ladder and enter the shuttle slip. Once inside we'll close the internal hatches, board the Cousteau, and open the aft gate."

A short climb through a tightly drawn circular hatch brought them into what looked like a low ceilinged airplane hangar. Alicia was struck by the smell of saltwater, and the heavy concentration of saline in the air stung her nostrils causing her to sneeze.

"Yes, no matter how I try, I just can't wash out all the salt. You'll get used to it in a minute."

Alicia focused ahead on the sleek craft resting on skids. It was compact, with a shape similar to that of a baleen whale. It had an almost flat top and somewhat widely arched lower section with large curved windows in the front. Two deeply cut slits in the flanks denoted the water intakes for the propulsion system. The stern came together in a large wing, again not unlike a whale's tale, that would give the vessel stability.

"Nice!" Alicia exclaimed.

"Thank you. It's forty feet long, has a beam of just twelve feet, and it sports two miniature versions of the propulsion unit that moves the Nautilus. I have to confess that those weren't standard equipment; I put those together and installed them during my last visit to dry dock. It's a hot rod," Nemo declared matter-of-factly.

"Boys will be boys," quipped Alicia.

"Oh really? As though mechanical power is merely a male pursuit! You know what they say?"

Surprised at this playful rebuttal, Alicia played along, "No, pray tell me, what do they say?"

"The smaller the woman, the larger the Sport Utility Vehicle."

"Oh do they? And just who are they, in any case?"

Nemo was laughing and kept on, "Come on, how many times have you been cut off by some little woman in a Hummer?"

Alicia had to admit to herself that there was some truth to this.

"Heck, you probably were the woman in the Hummer."

"No, no. I was the woman in the Porsche Cayman."

"The Cayman!?!" Nemo whistled shrilly, "Whoa! Well, excuse me. Perhaps Danica Patrick would like to board the Cousteau?"

"Only if I can drive!"

"What? Well, let me get it out of the garage and then you can unleash it in the open, okay?"

"Fair enough!"

Alicia followed Nemo up a ladder to a closed hatch in the underside. Nemo opened a small panel and typed in a code and the hatch slid open. Once they were both inside, Nemo touched a large orange button and the ladder automatically withdrew into the body of the vessel and the hatch slid shut and sealed. Another hatch also thudded into place. "What was that noise?" Alicia asked.

"Oh, for safety I always leave the external dive boot hatch open just in case I was caught in here and there was a malfunction with the outer gate and there was flooding."

The entryway was crowded with equipment and even though they could both stand upright, they had to angle their way forward. "I thought you said that this could hold a team of Special Forces soldiers."

"It could. Right now, though, I have the passenger area loaded with sonar equipment. Our purpose is to test the sonar eluding capacity of the Nautilus. We have the latest and most powerful active and passive systems aboard. In fact, Cousteau is a little on the heavy side. The extra power will come in handy just to maneuver. Have a seat on the left."

Alicia positioned herself into the well-padded seat and looked at the myriad of gauges before her. In the center was an extremely large compass and small gauge configuration. "Don't worry about all those gauges. Think of your Porsche. The one gauge that means anything is the tachometer that's dead center in the dashboard. The one gauge here that means anything is the compass. Once powered up, the compass will also become a viewfinder and navigation interface for dark, murky conditions. All set?"

Alicia nodded her head excitedly. Nemo reached over his head and toggled a switch. "This is the garage door opener," he chuckled. Instantly there was movement and Alicia could hear the sound of water rushing around the vessel. In less than a minute the water was making its way past the lower part of the curved glass. When it was half way up from the bottom, Nemo turned to Alicia, "You see that double lever on your left side near the wall? Pull both levers back; they open the venturis." Alicia did so and even before she had finished moving the levers, she could feel a slight vibration as the propulsion system started to work. An orange light that had been illuminated when they first boarded now changed to green. The water was now past the top of the cockpit's glass, and Alicia could clearly see the inside of the still illuminated slip.

"Alicia, the process for getting out is very easy. The top of the slip is sliding back into the hull of the Nautilus. I'm just going to gently squeeze the green button on the left side of my joystick."

"What? Wait, I can't see over your arm to the joystick in your right hand."

"Oh, right. Take the joystick in your right hand, then. Without pressing the green button, put your thumb over it. It is pressure sensitive, so you want to be very subtle until you get the hang of it." Nemo put his left hand over Alicia's and slowly but firmly closed her thumb against the button. The craft responded and began to lift off the deck. After a few seconds, he eased the pressure of his hand. "Okay, let go of the button. We're about eight feet off the deck. The craft will maintain whatever depth you set it to. Now, we're going to move backward."

He again placed his hand over hers and slowly moved the joystick back and instantly the vessel glided accordingly. "With a slight twist of the joystick, we can spin around. Good! Okay, forward is forward and the left to right movement is like any conventional joystick. The red pressure button on the right side of the stick operates just like the green except that it dives the vessel. Let's focus on even operation without diving. Okay, go for it!" Without hesitation, Alicia slammed the stick forward and the vessel began to shudder as the propulsion units churned within their housings. Alicia could feel herself being pressed into the seat and she noticed that the display in front of her began flashing various numbers, graphs, and then a row of red lights suddenly appeared on the top of the dashboard-like console.

"You're a maniac!" Nemo laughed loudly.

"What the hell happened!?!" Alicia shouted.

"You just went from zero to sixty knots in about eight seconds. If we hit even a shrimp at this speed it's all over. The red lights indicate that the systems are working at full capacity. The initial surge began to overheat the propulsion system at first; that was the graph that appeared. As the initial dead start load dissipated, the system was able to recover. Of course, at this speed, we're now about a mile from the Nautilus. Why don't you back off the throttle a bit and turn it around. No sudden turns! I've got a lot of special equipment aboard that isn't bolted down."

"Aye, sir!" Alicia teased and eased the stick to the port.

The Cousteau made a graceful arc and she noticed how the compass followed her motion and she brought it back around. "What's the blue triangle on the compass?"

"That's the Nautilus."

"I see. Can I make it dive?"

"Sure, take it gradually, though."

Alicia put the craft into a subtle slope and then popped the green button a couple times to bring it back up. She was having fun and Nemo enjoyed watching the expressions on her face as she deftly moved the vessel through an imaginary race course. She caught his stare from the corner of her eye and turned toward him.

"What is it?" she asked.

"Nothing," he nodded, still smiling.

She smiled broadly, too, and he thought her smile looked lovely despite the greenish hue cast by the panel lights.

"Okay. Slow up to a crawl and press the large square button over your head."

As she did so, the ocean around them lit up like a summer's day. The strong beams penetrated the liquid darkness and Alicia could make out the wing-like fins of the rear of the Nautilus.

"Raise the vessel so that we'll pass over the Nautilus with plenty of room to spare." Alicia looked through the curved glass that extended above her as well as below her and noticed the open slip which housed the Cousteau. The smooth dark skin of the Nautilus passed beneath and then the sail emerged as only a minute dorsal fin.

"Alright, stop us. Feather the stick back and forth until we register zero movement on the digital compass. Good." Nemo reached just in front of Alicia and pressed a blue button.

"That's a reset button for relative depth. The Nautilus will now serve as a bottom depth. So, take the Cousteau to two hundred feet above the Nautilus and hold it there."

"Right," Alicia responded, and as she put the craft in motion she peered through the curved bottom of glass as the Nautilus grew smaller but also longer. It was a beautiful, sleek ship; its form fully supported its function with nothing merely ornamental. In a few moments the required depth was met and the Cousteau stopped, suspended in liquid space.

"Why don't you stay here at the controls while I go back to conduct the tests? I'm going to suspend a sonar ball just below the interference of the Cousteau's thrusters and then run some comparisons with the new ballast modification deactivated and then activated." Without waiting for her to respond, Nemo left his chair and squeezed back through the cockpit entryway. Alicia looked around and tried to see into the darkness past the reach of the lights. For a moment, she paused and pushed herself back into the seat, afraid that the writhing shapes from the caldera would again appear. But there was no such danger. Only tiny shrimp-like creatures would occasionally come into focus. She soon lost interest and began to examine the various controls and gauges of the cockpit when Nemo called from the rear.

"Alicia?"

"Yes!" she yelled back.

"Take us down to one hundred feet above the Nautilus."

"Okay, now?"

"Yes, go ahead."

The Cousteau began to drop a bit too suddenly. "Easy!" Nemo shouted.

"What do I do?"

"Pump the green button until she slows to a stop and then start over again."

Alicia deftly worked the two buttons and in moments the Cousteau was stopped and hovering.

"We're at 89 feet," she called back.

"That's fine. I'll run the test from here."

For thirty minutes Alicia sat in her seat and stared into nothingness. She wondered about her future after this underwater excursion was finished. She thought of how she could return to the world as she had left it. There would be questions to be sure. She remembered Nemo's words about the Navy getting information from her one way or another. There would be interrogations, she corrected herself. What would she tell them? Would they trust her information? If she was considered tainted by the Department of Defense, her old job might not take her back. If they didn't take her back, if no news company would, then what? How would she live? Panic was taking hold of her, and she could feel perspiration beginning to surface on her scalp when she was interrupted by movement to her right. Nemo was settling himself into the other seat and she only heard half of what he had been saying.

"...So far so good. Conseil will run a number of analyses and we'll have a better— say, are you okay? You don't look so well."

"Hmm? Oh, I'm fine. You were saying something about it being all right?"

"Well, to a degree. Let's head back. Think you can park her?"

"Don't be silly," Alicia responded and was back on task.

Without further conversation, she expertly maneuvered her craft along the back of the Nautilus and smoothly slid into place.

The Cousteau was settling into its cradle when Alicia spoke, "Nemo, what is going to happen to me? You mentioned the Navy interrogating me. Won't they imprison me? Even if they don't, how will I earn a living? I doubt if the Post would take me back, and I don't think anyone else would either."

"Why do you say that? I would think that you would have instant celebrity status, money and fame and all that goes with it."

"Maybe. Or people might say that I colluded with a terrorist of the seas and put me in prison or more likely, Guantanamo Bay. Even if they didn't, no journalist could be fully trusted after something like this. 'Why am I not telling more?' 'What, my captor confined me to my cabin for however many weeks that will have passed?' That won't wash with the military. And I don't want to be interrogated." A tear rolled down her right cheek.

Nemo sat silent and motionless. She was right with regard to some of what she was saying. They both knew "interrogation" was a euphemism for what the Navy would do to her to recover information. He had thought he could set her off at some port with a bunch of money and fake identification and all would be fine. He wasn't seriously thinking of her future then as she was now doing, as they both needed to do. "Alicia, let's give it some time. Together we can figure out the details. I mean really, we're the two smartest people in this place, how can we not come up with a brilliant plan?"

Alicia smiled in spite of herself. The last of the water had drained from the bay and the large red signal light visible through the canopy had just turned green. Nemo rose and made his way back to the exit hatch.

27

Fishing

Nemo had given Conseil orders regarding the examination of the data and was making his way to the conn when Alicia appeared behind him. "Did you close the hatch on Cousteau?"

"No," came the laconic reply.

"Steward, make secure the Cousteau and double check all hatches for complete seal." "Aye, sir" responded the robot and it made straight for the aft section of the ship.

"Alicia, you'll be okay. We'll figure something out."

"I don't want to live my life on the run or anonymously, like in some kind of witness protection program."

"I understand. We could situate you in a Caribbean island nation and you could spend your days..."

"No, goddamn it! I don't want to be cut off from civilization. I want to be in the mix of things, as always."

Nemo was at a loss for words. Certainly, he understood her problem. Living among her fellow citizens but being unable to maintain her true identity was a type of suffocating death of who she is. Prowling the oceans ad infinitum was also unacceptable; he was solitary and stood aloof from the world, but she was a journalist, the quintessence of being one with the world, one who endeavors to make connections between all involved.

"Give it some time, Alicia. We might be able to make it look like you escaped and were marooned for some time. Or maybe fisherman could suddenly find you in a raft. I don't exactly know right now. If you want to leave, we'll make it our priority."

"No, there is more for me to see here. I just don't want to end up like you, an outcast from society and what's worse, hunted by powerful nations."

Nemo listened patiently. "I still don't see how that will happen. I'm as cynical as anyone when it comes to the United States' guarantees of protection and fairness. But really, though, you were not the one who destroyed a multi-billion dollar facility and irradiated whatever remains there were; you were not the one who stole a billion dollar submarine; and you did not kill U.S. servicemen. You stumbled across the person who did and, for whatever reason, he didn't kill you but held you against your will on board. As a newspaper I'd want exclusive rights to that story. The Navy can reasonably expect only so much information from you. They don't tell their own submarine crews where they are going, so why would I operate any differently?"

Alicia understood his point and though still skeptical, she was feeling better about her future.

"Now, can we please get some provisions on board before our next lunch?!?"

Alicia smiled broadly and then was once again interested in what lay ahead. "So how does one fish from a submarine?"

"Well, there are a couple of techniques. We can trail a net behind and scoop up an adequate amount or we can take someone else's catch by slicing open their nets and hauling in their catch."

"You actually steal other people's food? Starving people who need that source of protein!?!"

"Please, Alicia, those purse-seine nets destroy whole schools and mangle sea beds. And those fish aren't going to the poor; they're going to wealthy Japanese, American, or European tables. Jacques Cousteau demonstrated this beyond a doubt in his last book. Besides, I take only what I can reasonably use and let the rest go."

Alicia sat quietly, unconvinced.

"You read Cousteau and then we'll talk. Fair enough?"

"Sure, I've got time."

"That's the spirit!"

Moving fast and deep, the Nautilus sped toward the fishing grounds. Using sonar far more advanced than that equipping the fishing fleets above, Nemo targeted schools of fish that were not yet hedged in by the elaborate netting systems that lie in wait to snare their prize, like miles-long spider webs. The binding, unbreakable nylon afforded no chance of escape. As the fish followed their migratory route in one specific, unerring direction, the Nautilus approached from the oncoming direction trailing a net behind and above it like a kite. A single pass captured thousands of pounds of fish which were then hauled into the cargo area far aft. There, robots working in the partially flooded bay, opened the nets amidst the swimming, swirling bodies. When the nets were refolded, the process would begin again with a different catch as the target. In this manner and in only a half day, provisions were caught, butchered, and preserved. This tidy process disappointed Alicia who was expecting a laborious if not interesting process to observe. Nemo himself didn't even get his hands wet.

"So you thought I wore an apron and got in there with a fillet knife? Are you serious, with all this advanced robotic assistance, you want me to gut fish?" Nemo broke out in a genuine, hearty laugh.

"I just thought that you had more of a connection with the environment with what you're doing, especially after the sermon quoting your favorite prophet, Cousteau."

"How poetic! No, I like to concentrate on other matters. Besides, the inefficiency of my hands would result in spoilage."

"What do you mean?"

"Well, let's take a look at the crew doing this," Nemo offered.

Entering the cargo bay, Alicia was taken aback by what she saw. Some twenty robots were at work preparing the fish. The fish were piled according to species with four different piles, each comprising some half ton of fish. Two robots worked at each pile filleting and, where desired by Nemo, skinning the fish, while others were gutted. The speed and precision of their arms and hands was nothing short of amazing. While these pairs worked, other pairs rinsed and wrapped the fish for flash-freezing. At one table various liquids were being added to the bags of fish prior to sealing.

"What are those liquids?" asked Alicia.

"Oh, different marinades; I like some variety," explained Nemo.

Alicia nodded in agreement. All the while, ice was shoveled around and atop the fish to keep them fresh.

"As you can see, putting a knife in my hand would result in one preserved fish and probably twenty rotten ones!"

"I can't get over how fast their arms and hands move," Alicia marveled.

"Their movements are programmed, of course. Some robots, like DOC, can use their logic boards to figure out more efficient combinations. That's why DOC is so impressive in combat mode. His ability to react, to apply the most efficient action, and to pivot and bend in ways that are not possible for the human body to move, along with his alloy body make him unbeatable."

"Why do you call him DOC?" Alicia asked.

"It's an acronym for Directive Occupational and Combat unit. The directive aspect is that unless programmed otherwise, it only takes orders from one person; it also means that the unit takes a primary position in coordinating other robotic crew. That's why you may have noticed that the others obey DOC when he comes on to the scene. The occupational portion was originally programming that was to be determined by need. There were several DOC units in use during the building of the Nautilus. Some were devoted to welding and inspection; others were used for electrical and electronic installation—even clerical needs, which were very real on a project this large. My unit is a medical unit, adept at first aid and even surgery.

The military wanted all of the robots to have some defensive capability. Even the steward, who seems to be only for setting the table and pouring tea, is capable enough to defend against a dozen armed men without difficulty. You see how efficient the hands of these standard service robots are. Well, for DOCs, that defensive ability had to also include considerable offensive logic and the wherewithal to carry out an attack. In the event that terrorists infiltrated the construction area, the combat mode of the several units could, in a coordinated manner, quash such overt sabotage. My unit is the only survivor and has, since our departure from that base, undergone several modifications that have only worked to enhance already formidable abilities."

Alicia nodded and took in all that Nemo said. She thought of how she had earlier decided not to chance an attack on DOC and appreciated her restraint at that moment.

"So, Alicia, have you had enough aroma and scents of the sea here in our butchery? How about something to eat before our next stop for groceries?"

"What next stop?"

"Well, haven't I been saying that I need more champagne?"

28
What Luxury Is

Alicia ate heartily; the savory chowders that were assorted on the table and the fillets prepared in different ways brought an approving moan with every bite. Nemo chuckled at her appetite.

"What? What's so funny?"

"Nothing, I just find your appetite amusing. I like a woman who can eat. It's just amusing to find one who is somewhat petite put it away so easily."

"How did you come by this odd sense of humor over what others eat?"

"Oh, my wife could out-eat any three large men when it came to seafood. We'd go out to a restaurant and I'd order the largest platter they offered and then she would do the same. I couldn't finish my dessert, so she would finish it for me!"

Alicia smiled as she was caught off guard by this reference to his wife. She listened and restrained herself from asking other questions abut his wife. Pushing Nemo on such matters seemed to upset the emotional balance that was precariously maintained.

"We've stocked up on fish and that is the most important commodity. I like my luxury items, though, and I wasn't kidding about needing more champagne. About three months ago a luxury super yacht went down in a storm about 80 miles off the coast of Japan. She sank in about 1500 feet of water. The cost of recovering items from the wreck would not only be unreasonably high, the insurance money probably more than compensated the owner. Chances are what was aboard is still aboard. The wealthy, I have found, often have superb taste. We're going to see what we can gain. At least a couple cases of champagne have to be in the galley!"

"Are you doing this yourself or can I help?"

"Certainly, I thought you might enjoy the opportunity to do something other than pace the salon."

"That's true enough!" Alicia agreed. "How do you do it? Stay down here all the time? Every day, though offering some interesting study, no doubt, isn't much different from the day before or the day to follow."

Nemo considered her comments, but answered quickly, "In that respect I don't believe that life here is much different from life on land. However, I don't have any pressure to conform to others' standards or perform to someone else's expectations. If I want to study history, art, the teeming varieties of oceanic fauna and fish and mollusks, I can do that as long and as thoroughly as I want. The research need not be practical; it can be pure research which is often the most liberating."

"That's not to say that I haven't made practical tools from observing nature's perfection," Nemo explained. "Take the squid, for example. When it hunts, it uses its tentacles to grasp its prey and then, using both its motion and the grip of those tentacles, it pulls the prey and itself together; its arms then take the prey the rest of the way. I have a defensive anti-torpedo weapon that works along the same principle. A bullet-shaped projectile is fired in the direction of the oncoming torpedo. The projectile, which is only about half the length and weight of a conventional torpedo, is rocket propelled. Its speed is about that of the Barracuda that we talked about before. It homes in on the torpedo and closes ground before any avoidance can take place. About fifteen meters from the torpedo, a titanium link chain with numerous grappling surfaces fans out and when any one of the grapplers makes contact, the chain is retracted and the projectile is drawn into the path of the torpedo where it is detonated. Even if the explosive within the projectile fails, the collision of the two as well as the added encumbrance of the projectile nullifies the torpedo. I call it the Red Devil, after the fierce red squid off the coast of Mexico."

"Did you use these Red Devils when we were being attacked?"

"No, I didn't need to. The sea floor was uneven enough and there were outcroppings of rock that the torpedoes clipped, thereby detonating them."

"Oh. That's nice," Alicia nervously replied. The thought of dying in the depths unnerved her and Nemo's chatter about his high-tech equipment was disturbing. He, himself, had admitted that he didn't always think in terms of actual cost or experience, just chance and probabilities. He was going on about his inventions as though they were prized horses or dogs. He seemed to her to be poised for a conflict. She did not believe that the conflict would be with her, but rather, some nemesis on the surface or hunting him in the depths. She had once believed that he was dispassionate, but she was reminded yet again that it was quite the opposite case. She again realized this could be disastrous for her.

"So, anyway," continued Nemo, "the yacht that went down in 1500 feet of water should provide some treats. Aside from champagne, I'm thinking of sculptures, jewelry, even some extra parts."

"Fifteen hundred feet seems dangerous."

"Well, any dive can be dangerous; it's true. But our dive suits are good for a thousand meters. There is a transparent half-helmet that we'll wear to protect our sinus cavities and facial bone structure. Your gloves will be replaced by tiny, web-like chain mail made of mimetic alloy to protect your hands."

"Well, I have to say that as nervous as I was before, the experience was thrilling!"

"Good. I'm glad. We'll be in the vicinity in about half an hour. You might want to use the restroom and make your way to the dive boot. I'll be back there shortly after I finalize some programming for the scavenging crew."

29
SMASH AND GRAB

"You can't be serious!" Nemo huffed, as he stared at the screen displaying the forward scanners' data. Alicia had just come up the stairs into the conn.

"What's going on? I thought we were going to dive this wreck."

Nemo glanced at her and then pointed at the movement on the screen. There a deep sea submersible hovered just to the port of the wrecked yacht, its robotic arms moving within the light cast by the rack of high beam projectors hanging from the sub's superstructure. The effect was not unlike the silhouette of a spider. Every once in a while a bright sparking would illuminate the side of the yacht.

"Guess you've been beaten to the prize," Alicia pronounced with a trace of mockery in her voice.

"They're reclaiming their loss," Nemo mechanically said.

"How do you know that they are the owners?"

"True. Well, whoever they are, they aren't going to pillage my wreck."

"What!?! Your wreck! How do you figure it's your wreck!?!" Alicia sharply questioned.

"Everything under the surface is mine. It's simply so." Alicia stared at him, unbelieving. "This is my domain, as I've explained before. I am unbothered by what those at the surface do. Taking their actions beneath the waves matters not. That wreck is mine and those contents shall furnish my gallery and stock my galley. Now, if you will excuse me, I need to clear out these interlopers before they clean me out." Nemo strode past Alicia and as he did so he commanded, "DOC, battle mode. Battle stations! Secure for silent running."

Alicia was dumbfounded. She wanted no part of what was about to happen. Nemo wasn't, however, asking her to join him now. She turned around and called after him, "I am not getting involved with this!"

"No one asked you to. I don't care what you do. Stay in the conn or go wherever you want. The steward will attend you."

This final statement resounded within her: 'the steward will attend you.' She was being kept under guard. Although she moved aboard as a passenger, she was still, in fact, a prisoner, enabled to move about her cell as she had originally exclaimed. "I'll be in my room," Alicia called back. Nemo made no reply.

Outside the yacht, the submersible had just removed the four large panels of the hull that were cut out by the remotely controlled cutting torch. The operator confirmed that the interior was now accessible. The sub's pilot was just radioing the information to the ship at the surface when his radio cut out along with the cabin lights. Then the bank of outer lights went out and the torch no longer functioned. Within the sub, panic was taking hold of the two operators. Nemo and Ulysses patiently waited as the crew members ran through a few different procedures to try to restore power. Nemo watched from behind the sub as the flickering of a flashlight occasionally darted from within the submersible. A moment later, Ulysses moved behind the sub's two propellers, and taking aim with both lasers, began burning perforations into the propeller blades. At the very least, the holes would render the sub much less maneuverable. At the worst, the propellers would eventually crack and shear off with the spinning of the drive shafts. The sub would make it to the surface, but recovery would be difficult and very time consuming.

Just as the last burn was completed, the submersible began to ascend and as it did so, the propellers came to life. Ulysses was gently pushed back by the thrust. The sub moved forward at once, but as soon as Ulysses' considerable bulk was farther away and could no longer serve as a point of resistance for the wash of the propellers, the sub slowed to a pathetic, wobbling progression. Ascending to the surface would not be a problem, but negotiating the currents farther above would be frustrating. At some point the submersible would blow its ballast and rise to the surface to be recovered. At the surface the hand held radios would be operating and the ship above would have to move out to recover its drifting white bobber, a time consuming process under the best of conditions.

Without hesitation, Nemo and his crew went to work. Twenty robots coordinated in pairs and armed with laser cutters, moved on and around the Delta yacht lying on its side. With deliberate, patient work, the yacht was dissected into sections between ten and fifteen feet and length. Each segment was loaded onto a sled that was equipped with ballast tanks and thrusters that maintained neutral buoyancy, even as weight was added. In little more than an hour, the 120 foot vessel had been sectioned and loaded and was now being packed into the cargo bay of the Nautilus.

The mighty engines and drive trains of the luxury vessel were all that remained. Ulysses circled just above the bit of hull and the bulkheads that cradled the machinery; they were the last signs that a large, elegant yacht had been there just a little while before. He held an immense cone shaped piece of equipment that was rigged with its own floats to make for easier handling. As he circled, a thick, almost chunky looking light broke from the bottom of the cone. It was a laser far more powerful than any of the other instruments that had been used to penetrate the hull of the Delta. This was not a precision instrument, but a blunt excavation tool. The seabed burned and gasses were escaping in blinding clouds as the crust which had easily supported the weight of the sunken vessel was now being boiled away.

Ulysses angled the beam of the laser so that it would reach farther to the center of the circle he had just traced. He worked his way around, his sensors unbothered by the debris and clouds of gas. After about fifteen minutes the ground began to sag and the remainder of the engine room began to sink. Moments later the entire unit fell through and embedded into the molten hole ten feet beneath the seabed. Just then, a sledge with several tons of rock and sediment slid alongside the pit. Ulysses transmitted several commands and the two robots attending the sledge moved into position and tipped the contents into the still smoking crater. With that, it was over; the resting place of the yacht was no more, just another area along the millions of miles of seafloor of the Sea of Japan.

30

The Lion's Share

As Nemo looted the other guy's bounty, Alicia reflected upon Nemo's inexplicable mood swing, from cavalier bon vivant to deliberate thief and terrorist. She fumed over his behavior and wondered at his assigning her an escort. This latter action wounded her, and this riled her anger. How could she have let herself enjoy his company for even a minute? How could she be so naïve as to think that her time spent aboard was more a pleasant excursion than a prison sentence? Her journalistic instincts piqued, she reviewed her usual process of analysis. To understand either victim or victimizer, one must walk in that individual's shoes and down the paths that led to the present.

Nemo was wounded; he felt betrayed but yet felt guilty all the time. His one possession was the Nautilus and his life aboard it. Again, the issue of time was central. Whatever time he had left, he was determined to enjoy, and he liked his creature comforts, his luxuries. The twist, though, is that he considers everything beneath the waves his. The water is inseparable from time and time was his. The other excavation crew were competitors, nothing more. She wondered if they, like the crew of the narcotics laden trawlers, were now part of the food chain.

The logic was valid, though nonetheless chilling, and it genuinely frightened her. The moment he ever got it into his head that she might be part of that competition, it was over for her. This took the charm out of his smile, his conversation, and his gifts from forgotten galleons. As for her brother's watch and the satisfying act of vengeance? Well, it didn't make sense unless Nemo was trying to purchase her trust. But for what end? It wasn't sex; it wasn't for scientific collegiality; and the simple answer of companionship wasn't possible because they both agreed that her stay was limited. She actually delayed her departure when he offered her passage home before they entered the Sea of Japan. Why would Nemo take her aboard, even having to go through the trouble of saving her life, if only to have a few conversations? Perhaps this was all there was behind it after all.

Alicia was troubled about the fate of the crew within the submersible and wanted answers. She opened her room's door and the steward came to life.

"Ma'am?"

"Where's Nemo?"

"The Captain is in the cargo bay, sorting supplies."

"I'd like to see him, now."

"Of course, follow me."

The walk seemed to take forever as the cargo bay was nearly four hundred and fifty feet of twisting corridors and stairways behind her cabin. Outside the entrance the steward ushered her in. As she stepped through the small service hatch, her eyes were dazzled by the bright lighting and the flurry of movement within.

The cargo area was large, wide, and sloped toward the aft part of the submarine. She couldn't believe her eyes. Sections of the yacht's hull were stacked near the rear and were draped with an enormous net made of heavy chains. Neatly arranged piles were positioned on the floor; some contained nothing but bright silver hardware like hand pulls for drawers and doors. Another pile contained plates and stemware; another was cookware. There were at least two dozen such groupings and robots were working at some of these, carefully packing crates with the valuable objects. It wasn't until Alicia had visually swept the entire cargo bay that she noticed Nemo sitting upon a high stool at an elevated desk in a corner parallel to where she stood.

He didn't see her at first, and as she approached, Alicia noticed cheap half-glasses perched upon the end of his nose and he was making notations in a book. She could tell that he was aware of her appearance, but did not avert his gaze from the open ledger page. Alicia wasted no time with niceties. "Well, Nemo, are the crew members of that submarine feasting the fishes?"

"You actually think that I killed people over some spare parts and a few cases of wine?"

"Well, didn't you?"

Nemo laughed ruefully and looked out over the work that was efficiently progressing before him. He took the glasses off and twirled them by one of the arms. "Alicia, please, please!" He turned toward her and she could see the fatigue that ringed his eyes and paled his coloring. "I don't kill people over a few minor material objects. Their sub was disabled, it's true, but they were in no danger, just some stress. They couldn't see and they couldn't navigate much, if at all. Their life support systems and ballast function were left intact. They're probably sleeping in their bunks right now, exhausted from debriefings and paperwork."

Alicia considered this but was still angry with Nemo. "Still, you had no right to do what you did."

"And did they have a right to do what they were attempting? If they were the rightful owners, they were defrauding the insurance company. Believe me, no underwriter would consider a yacht sunken in 1500 feet of water to be anything but a complete loss; the policy had been paid out. Recovering valuable items after being compensated for them is fraud. If they weren't the owners, then they were no better than I. The difference, though, is that they were using inferior equipment and chance was not with them today. Damn it!" Nemo threw his glasses across the desk and called out, "Conseil!" From among the robots on the floor, Conseil hastened to his master's voice. As he approached, he recognized Alicia, "Good day, ma'am." Alicia nodded.

"Conseil, transcribe these entries into the main database and see that the stowage is properly completed. I want to be able to leave the vicinity in about three hours."

"Very good, sir. It shall be completed well within your time requirement."

Nemo hopped off his stool and walked past Alicia without saying anything.

"Where are you going?" Alicia asked.

Nemo stopped, and turning toward her, he distinctly pronounced the words and paused after each, as though he were speaking to an idiot: "Wherever I please!" He spun on his heel and crouched through the service hatch and was gone. Alicia and Conseil stood for a moment staring at the opening as if expecting Nemo to reappear. He was already halfway to the Turkish bath when they turned away.

31
REFLECTION

After Nemo's departure, Alicia was about to follow him but reconsidered. Instead, she walked about the cargo area looking over the various items that were being packed. Three cases of Dom Perignon stood out as well as two cases of Chateau Lafite Rothschild. Beside these cases, an acrylic tray on a collapsible table unceremoniously displayed several watches along with some earrings and a string of pearls. Alicia picked through the objects: a Vacheron Constantin men's watch, a Zenith dive watch, and a Van Cleef bracelet. "Nice haul," Alicia remarked to herself with arched eyebrows. Were it not for her ethical objections, she would have been excited about these objects and would have even asked him for one of them. But none of these items could be legitimately claimed; she wanted none of this sordid bounty.

She knew, however, that no matter how righteous her actions, she occupied a social order with expected conventions of giving and taking, even at the bottom of the ocean with one other person. Alicia was confident that Nemo would assist her in departing; that is, as long as she stopped questioning his motives and betraying disapproval of his actions. It would be a clean break, but not until after diving the Titanic. Yes, then she would take her leave of the good captain. She would not mention this last uncomfortable exchange, just act as though nothing happened.

As Alicia toured this impromptu flea market, Nemo was receiving a vigorous massage to work out the knots and cramps of his stressed body. The steward expertly worked the kinks in Nemo's upper back, applying just the right pressure to break the resistance and smooth the tissues. As the robot worked, Nemo did not permit his mind to consider any problems or even coherent ideas; he emptied his consciousness of any stressors. Slowly, his aching body relaxed and he let himself go limp. "Captain?" interrupted the mechanical masseur.

"Yes?"

"If I may say so, I detect quite a build up of lactic acid and your perspiration demonstrates an abundance of caffeine and nicotine. I might suggest rehabilitative hydration."

"Yes, that's very good. I am thirsty. Prepare the usual dosage and I'll take it now."

"Yes, sir."

In addition to the healing properties of the minerals that constantly swirled in the baths, Nemo had formulated a tonic of sorts that not only rehydrated one, but employed natural salts that attracted toxins like a magnet. Two liters of this drink would be all that was necessary to purify one's system; the contaminants were released during urination. The steward brought an icy pitcher and tumbler and Nemo sat up, propping himself on one arm. He drank deeply and drained a tall glass and afterward handed it back for refilling. After finishing the second glass, he lay down and the steward resumed the massage where he left off.

An hour later, Nemo was immersing himself in the mineral water bath. He permitted himself to think, and the first genuine thought that occupied him was that the mineral bath was his greatest discovery. He could feel vitality seeping into his weary frame. He let himself slide in over his head. After holding his breath for a half minute, he exhaled and poked his head above the bubbling surface. He made his way to the edge where the steward had left the remaining restorative water in the pitcher with the glass. Nemo greedily drank some more and perched his shoulders on the edge, kicking his legs out before him. He tipped his head back and looked up at the tiled octopus that reached down to him. As he let his mind range over various thoughts, he paused; a smile, ever so slight, spread across his lips.

32
Turning the Page

Alicia made her way to the salon when she was intercepted by a steward. "Ma'am, are you seeking the Captain?" So, she was still being watched.

"Yes, as a matter of fact, I am."

"He is working in the museum of technology which is just off the gallery. Follow me." Alicia wondered if the robot had been spying or was simply being the good maître'd. She realized that is was pointless to try to "read into" the actions of a machine. As they walked, the steward continued, "Would you care for some refreshment?" As Alicia was about to answer they turned a corner into the room in which Nemo was working. Nemo interrupted, "I recommend the tuna sandwich and sea chips with a pint of some homemade ale. It's a working woman's lunch." He stood there smiling at her. Alicia was taken aback by the tremendous change of mood that had taken place. Not only was there no trace of the irritation that punctuated their last exchange, Nemo looked refreshed, almost younger. In contrast to his usual loose fitting tunic, relaxed pants and slipper boots, he was wearing bright blue coveralls and thick-soled, black work shoes. After a pause, Alicia replied, "Tuna it is! But can I have some soup, too?"

"Make that two."

"Yes, right away!" With that, the robot scurried off.

"So, this is the museum of technology?"

"Yes, and it's also a work room. Technical artifacts exist here from disciplines as diverse as hydrodynamics, electrical engineering, naval architecture, even watch making! I also keep the attendant library of schematics and performance analyses here as well."

Alicia walked about the room. The space was somewhat cramped with large worktables, blueprint cabinets, and a large drafting table, all organized in a semicircle some fifteen feet in diameter. Around the perimeter of the room were glass display cabinets containing various objects. Alicia admitted that she didn't know what half these objects were or why they were significant to warrant a place under the glass. Just as she finished her turn around the room, lunch arrived on trays. "Have a seat," Nemo said as he pulled a drafting chair to the edge of the table where he sat.

"So what brings us into the technical room?" Alicia asked as she bit into her grilled sandwich.

"Well, we're diving the Titanic and every dive on the Titanic is first and foremost, a technical challenge. Though not the deepest wreck, its depth would crush even our mimetic alloy dive suits. It's freezing cold; the wreck itself is extremely hazardous and nearly every hands-on action raises clouds of silt. We're not interested in plundering a wreck as we did with the galleon. We want merely to observe this sanctuary, this graveyard of the dreams, the aspirations of those," he paused and swallowed hard, "those lost, but who continue to remind us of their times and their last moments among us."

Alicia said nothing and awkwardly resumed chewing, not having realized she had stopped as Nemo spoke.

"In any case, it's dangerous and getting worse every year."

"Why?"

"As I mentioned briefly before, there are iron devouring bacteria that suck the iron out of the steel and thus weaken the whole structure. That ship was stressed to the highest degree when it broke up and especially when it crashed into the seabed at some fifty miles per hour. The fact that it has held together at all ought to refute those who claim that her steel was defective. Everything is relative. Most modern steel is inferior to mimetic alloy, but that does not mean it can't be used to make for robust construction. In any case, Titanic is being eaten away and one must keep in mind that the structures that support the decking and the walls are still supporting tons and tons of weight. A minor mishap weakening one area could jeopardize the whole. Anyone caught in that collapse would perish. For this reason, I'm telling you that you need not dive this. It's no skin off your nose or wound to pride. Without exaggeration, I can honestly say that this trip will constitute the most dangerous wreck dive ever made, period."

Alicia took a long draft of her beer. "I understand, really. I want to make this dive."

"You're absolutely sure?"

"Yes."

"You'll cooperate with my instructions entirely?"

"Yes."

"I'm serious, there's no room for error here or independent judgment."

"Yes! Yes! A thousand times yes!" Alicia exclaimed.

"Very well."

With that, they finished their lunch in a silence not born of antagonism, but engagement in a common goal. As the last of the chips were consumed and the pickled sea urchin was crunched away, coffee was brought and the planning commenced.

33
Some Technical Considerations

Alicia began by bringing up something Nemo had just mentioned about water pressure. "You said the alloy suits would be crushed. How, then, do we dive at this depth if the suits fail?"

"Right. Diving the Titanic had always been a goal of mine. I was never happy with the small remote robotic devices that broadcast video of the various decks and debris fields. I wanted to be there and see it with my own eyes and handle things with my own hands. For this reason, uniquely designed dive suits were in order." Nemo reached into his left breast pocket and produced a pack of cigarettes and an old, dented, Zippo lighter. "Smoke?"

"Sure," Alicia accepted. Nemo tapped a cigarette from the pack and Alicia withdrew it and as she did so, she palmed the lighter. Nemo found himself a cigarette and held out his hand for the lighter.

"I wasn't going to steal it," Alicia protested. Once replaced in his palm, he lit up and dropped the lighter into his pocket.

"I mean I can't say I wasn't tempted given how nice it is," she teased.

"A gift from my father," Nemo returned and resumed his disquisition.

"I just want to clarify something you said earlier," a voluminous cloud exhaled across the table, moving toward Alicia, "the mimetic alloy suits at their present specification could not withstand the water pressure at nearly two and a half miles below the surface, some six thousand pounds per square inch. More accurately, we, within the suits, would be crushed. A thicker and therefore more resilient caliber of alloy could, however, withstand the pressure. The problem, though, is that the suit's mass and weight would require Herculean strength to operate within it. A negative pressure field such as the Nautilus uses would be even more ungainly."

"What? What's a negative pressure field? In plain English, Nemo."

"Sorry. One of the reasons the Nautilus can dive to great depths is because as the propulsion system operates to propel the vessel, it also is directed to form a barrier against the pressure of the water outside the hull. The force of the outside pressure is, to a degree, counteracted by the pressure exerted outward from within the hull. Again, there are limits to this process. The sea always wins these contests eventually. In any case, such a system requires too much material to make for an effective dive suit.

The common denominator here is that humans can't deal with these depths and with these materials, so I thought, 'why not make oneself a robot?' Using a couple extra DOC frames, I designed an articulated exoskeleton of sorts. We wear the suit, which utilizes the heavy gauge mimetic alloy, but the heavy lifting is done through electrical motors and servos that respond to our movements. For example, we might take a couple steps forward standing here in this room with very little effort on our total musculature. In heavy gauge alloy, each step would weigh about four hundred pounds. With electromechanical assistance, that differential can be brought back to our experience of walking here in the study. For this reason, there is no problem of coordination or equilibrium."

"Impressive," commented Alicia, "but wouldn't we hopelessly sink with that kind of weight?"

"Yes, absolutely. That's why the suit is equipped with flotation that creates a negative buoyancy."

"Well, Nemo, it seems that you have figured out all the angles again. This seems fairly safe. Why all the reassurances of whether I want to go through with this?"

Nemo ground out his cigarette into the elegant oyster shell that had served as an ashtray. "The suit doesn't make you invincible; it merely enables you to survive an environment that would ordinarily crush you flat. Think of yourself as a baby who has been placed into the backseat of a car. Sure, you're safer than if you were outside of the car. Now park that car over a railroad track. If a slow passenger train stops in time, a fatal wreck might be avoided. If a speeding freight train hits the car, the baby will succumb, despite the relative safety of the backseat. The Titanic is the slow passenger train; it's dangerous but maybe not fatal today. It is also the freight train. If even minor structural components are compromised, thousands of tons will fall upon you. The suit will have meant nothing. Resilience to water pressure is only one problem."

"One of the limitations of my breathing technology," Nemo continued, "is that the gill system we use depends upon a fairly clean environment. Titanic kicks up an incredible amount of silt. This clogs the gill and cannot be easily cleaned out in the lab, let alone on a dive. We could quite easily choke to death. I've created filters that utilize water pressure to comb out debris and I've rerouted the water intakes and even equipped the suit with a spare tank of water to be used for breathing. The fact, though, is that a cloud of silt is going to break the equipment, regardless. Our suits will contain an additional gill that can be snapped into place, but it requires dexterity and the ability to hold one's breath in a stressful environment. During the change out of a gill, nitrogen narcosis is a very real threat."

Alicia stared at him through the dissipating cloud of smoke and said nothing. Satisfied with her silence, Nemo rose from his seat and approached one of the blueprint cabinets. Without hesitation he opened one of the lower drawers and pulled out several large prints of schematics and drawings.

"Right," he began as he took his place again atop the stool. "I have two sets of drawings of the Titanic, a 'before' and 'after' perspective, if you will. Currently, this is the state of the bow section and these bright green arrows indicate previous points of entry for various prior expeditions. Given the limited technology, the various companies did a fine job. Now, this is where I have proceeded." Nemo pulled another drawing from the pile and placed it on top of the first one. A dark red arrow traced a path through an area of mud and furrowed seabed plowed up as high as the anchors. Below the surface level of the mud, a jagged, darkened cutout was traced upon the hull. "The black jagged space represents a puncture of about four feet across in the peak tank of the lower orlop deck." Alicia quizzically turned to him and raised her left hand in an expression of uncertainty.

"Pardon me," Nemo politely responded, "the peak tank is a small tank in the bow or stern of a ship that is sometimes used for storage of liquids like potable water in the case of a liner or cruise ship. Accounts of some of the crew on that night mention air escaping from the peak tank. The orlop is one of the lowest decks on the ship. Only the decking that covered the ballast tanks and supported the boilers and engines, known as the tank top, was lower than the orlop. The Titanic's bow is plowed into the seabed quite deeply. As I said before, the usual theories of how she sank and the time frame given never satisfied me. Though the grounding theories are valid, and Edward Wilding's remains the best, I figured that there had to be more to the story in terms of damage." Nemo took a drag from his cigarette and then crushed it out in a black shell ashtray.

"Simply stated, Ulysses and I excavated the seabed near the peak tank and there it was: a ragged hole about four feet across at its widest point. I swam right in and found myself in an open space. Although a lot of decking had been destroyed, the front part of the ship had quickly filled with water and so the pressure was equalized when she sank. This is why the bow didn't break apart even as it slid into the seabed with such force. The third class cabins up front had miraculously remained intact. Boiler number six, which is situated on a parallel axis with the bridge, did not tear off. It provided an effective barrier when debris was hurled forward as the Titanic tilted upright and then quickly broke in two."

"Incredibly, the cargo in the bow did not entirely go crashing forward, partly because it was secured and partly because ice that had broken through the double hull and penetrated into the cargo hold provided a barrier."

"Ice in the hold?" Alicia incredulously interrupted.

"As I was saying, I entered the hole in the peak tank and the inside of that tank had been blown out. As I shone my light down, I could see what appeared to be two ruts on either side of the keel with a wide point of entry and gradual narrowing. The slit open steel acted like a cheese grater, slicing out a considerable section of ice. The bulkhead just aft of the peak tank was collapsed."

"Amazing!" Alicia said, genuinely impressed. "Will we be diving this section?"

"Sure, if you want. We'll need to re-excavate the areas; I covered my tracks. I thought, however, you might want to see more of the interesting, more celebrated areas of the wreck." Alicia turned from the drawing and looked directly into Nemo's eyes, "You mentioned human remains. Everyone has said that there are none." Nemo returned her gaze and then turned his eyes downward and reached into his pocket again for another cigarette. He lit up, inhaled, and blew the smoke to the side and back, turning his head with the same sort of motion a swimmer uses when inhaling.

"The remains are mostly in the third class berths at the bow and in the area of boiler number six. The ice cold water and the lack of current have precluded the typical decomposition or consumption by microorganisms; the sealed area kept out any other marine life as well. The corpses are wonderfully preserved. Their clothes, what they held on to, the horrible mask of asphyxiation...all present." Nemo took a long drag from his cigarette. "There are others in the stern section and skeletal remains in the mud flat just ahead and off the starboard side of the stern. The thing about human bones is that they don't cling to pleasant trinkets like tea cups and portmanteaux." Nemo bitterly bit the stub of the cigarette in two. Alicia pretended not to notice Nemo's disgust.

"Well, as I understand it, a number of tributes and plaques have been placed on the wreck," Alicia reminded him.

"True. What of it? They appear as not much more than refrigerator magnets. They are cheap and cluttered and do nothing but litter the burial ground."

"In your opinion" Alicia challenged him.

"Yes, in my opinion," Nemo quickly shot back. "Tell me if you retain your tolerance after the dive."

She was about to respond when she remembered her plan of not causing friction and alienating the man.

"Yes, we'll see," she conceded, "what, though, of these other celebrated areas of the wreck?"

As Alicia moved on, so did Nemo. "Well, there are the upper decks which still retain some of their grandeur. Some of the more deeply carved woodwork is still intact and even some portions of the Parisian café and Turkish bath are in order. The first class cabins can be gone through. A few bureaus contain jewelry, pictures, mementos."

"Amazing! I suppose you won't permit me to bring any of these artifacts back on board?"

"Let your conscience guide you, Alicia, and you won't go wrong."

She thought of this remark made cryptic by this man who followed his conscience which had been mangled and deformed. Her reflection was cut short by the mechanical voice of a robot speaking through Nemo's wrist interface.

"Sir, we are at the target site and are approaching a canyon of nearly 1700 feet. Shall we jettison the yacht's remains as we pass over the deepest part?"

"Affirmative."

Alicia arched her eyebrows and Nemo explained, "The only remains of that yacht are the engines and drive systems that are buried under ten feet of silt. The partitioned hull will be in an abyss many miles away."

"Oh, how long until we're at the Titanic?"

"Well, we're going to take our time. I need to reconnoiter a fifty mile radius and determine the best means of approach. Also, you need some practice in the new dive suit and I want to run some tests on you to determine how quickly your body rids itself of lactic acid." Alicia couldn't help herself this time, "What the hell for? You're not performing any tests on me!"

"Like I said, the suit only does so much," Nemo calmly replied, "you will still be moving through a thick medium and the bulk of the apparatus is considerable. To compensate for its weight, the electric motors assist your movement; they don't do it for you. There is a fatigue factor. As I said before, if you have to change out a gill, you need to be able hold your breath, snap it in and then rid your body of toxins that can impair you physically as well as mentally."

34
HUSHED TONES

For three days, Alicia submitted to various blood tests, cardio fitness tests, and training in the suit. She had just finished a light workout under the direction of Conseil and an evaluation by DOC. She was now resting on the chaise lounge in the darkened salon when Nemo entered, followed by the steward who was pushing a dessert trolley and coffee service.

"So, DOC tells me that you are quite the athlete."

Alicia sat up on the edge of the cushion, "Yeah, right. I took my medicine; do I get a treat now?"

"That's the idea."

"How about a cigarette; the usual assortment has been removed."

"Sorry, but no. Like in the caldera, it isn't a good idea to put an additional load on your vascular system. Even though the suits are effective, the body still knows it's in an unusual environment."

"You make it sound like we're going to the moon."

"Essentially, we are. In its own way, the bottom of the Atlantic is every bit as dangerous as the moon. —Scone?" Nemo offered.

Alicia rose and helped herself at the tray while Nemo poured out two cups of coffee. Both took their treats and sat themselves at the table and began to eat without saying anything.

"So, where were you during my trials in the puppeteer's seat?"

"I had to make some preparations for the dive. I wanted to make sure the lighting systems and the gear were in order. I always do it twice by myself and then Conseil checks it over." Alicia nodded absently. "So where are we?" Nemo focused and locked her eyes with his, "We are here."

The salon went black. Alicia couldn't see anything, not even Nemo who was sitting just a few feet from her. "This is what it looks like at nearly thirteen thousand feet beneath the surface at noon." Alicia strained her eyes and waited for them to adjust to the conditions. "You're thinking that you'll get used to the darkness and be able to see something in a few moments, but you won't. Despite all that you heard about people having acute night vision if just given the time to adapt does not apply in these depths. This is the night of first nights, when the Atlantic had just been scooped out by the tectonic shifts brought on by the inner convulsions of a still young planet. This solitude is that of the grave, of the shadow that passes from the living sight to that of oblivion. This is the graveyard."

With this final comment Alicia was stunned and shielded her eyes from a scorching white light that filled the room. In a moment her eyes adjusted and she stared out the transparent curving wall of the observation panels. Before her, and rising far above into the darkness, was a wall of black with daubs of white and brownish orange growths sprouting from between empty spaces, spaces that she realized were portholes. This was Titanic. Nemo admired the still imposing hulk before them for a few moments and then turned to observe Alicia's reactions. She backed into the salon as if to better take in the picture before her, her mouth agape.

The rivets stood out in icy clearness, thousands of points, still holding fast the overlapping plates of steel, shingled like the skin of an enormous reptile. It was still powerful and sleek in the way that only black paint can conjure. The color was still true. Above the black line, a distinct white territory, the border now rust stained, began and pushed above into the black Atlantic sky of the ocean. A porthole hung precipitously open. A face could still have hung in that opening, waving adieu to well wishers at the dock. Was that a face now hanging back in the shadows made by the peering lights turned on the wreck?

"She's still majestic," Nemo offered. Alicia broke her reverie.

"My God! I...I didn't realize how large. I mean the videos all show only a...a boat, a broken boat in the mud."

"Well, that's the hubris of a film crew who thinks they've mastered the wreck."

Alicia ignored the comment. "How come we have never been shown it like this?"

"Because we're on the seabed, right next to her. Something they can't do without risk."

"So we aren't at risk?"

"Oh, I never said that. We could get mired in it; foul the propulsion system; hit buried debris; all sorts of possibilities. But nothing worthwhile comes without risk. Keep in mind that as high as her boat deck is above us, a height our lights haven't penetrated, her keel is below the sea floor." Alicia was genuinely dumbstruck and she walked like a somnambulist toward the curved glass. Nemo took a seat at the table and quietly reached for his cup of coffee and sipped.

After some minutes had passed, Alicia turned toward where Nemo sat.

"It's..."

"No less than archangel ruined," Nemo interrupted, having read her thoughts.

"Yes," she concluded, "that's it exactly."

"Only Milton can speak clearly enough. We merely attend the sight, speaking with blind mouths."

"I have not thought of Milton since a stuffy course in literature a long time ago," Alicia reflected, "and you're right; only that kind of epic verse is appropriate." She paused, "Can we see any other part or must we stay here?"

"Let me give you a sense of Titanic's size," Nemo responded, turning his attention to the interface on his wrist. "Conseil?"

"Yes, Captain."

"Using only trim pulsers and battery power only—I repeat, battery power only— take us a hundred feet next to the exposed reciprocating engine in the aft section."

"Aye, sir!"

Immediately, Alicia could feel the floor of the salon vibrate ever so slightly and a yellowish tinged cloud began to make its way up the salon's observation panel. "The vibration you felt is from the Nautilus' skids breaking the suction of the mud. If we stayed here overnight we'd end up having to cut off the skids to get free." As Nemo explained, the vessel began to rotate and with its rotation, the cloud of silt disappeared from sight. The Nautilus then moved forward, slowly, even overcautiously. "The lighting is rigged on various points on the hull. If we move too fast, the lights will either implode or tear off." Alicia was reminded of something Nemo said earlier about when they would arrive at the sight.

"I thought you said that you had to wait and see before going to the wreck to get a sense of who else would be here."

"I did, but there is a category five storm raging at the surface and no one is sticking around. No tourist trade this week I can assure you."

It took a few minutes, but the Nautilus made its way down the two-thousand foot corridor of debris separating the two broken halves of the great ship. The Nautilus ceased its forward propulsion and drifted a bit before side thrusters sharply rotated the vessel to starboard.

"Conseil, nose us in so that the target is dead ahead."

"Aye, sir," came the quick reply.

The sleek fish answered the controls and wriggled into place.

"Set her down on the skids."

"Skids on contact, Captain."

"Well done."

"Yes, Captain!"

Nemo smiled at the robot's seeming sense of self worth. Nemo turned his attention again to the observatory where Alicia was already standing, looking up.

35
The Giant's Shoulders

Pointing out from among the shadows, now illuminated by the Nautilus' lighting rig, parts of machinery shone in hues of orange and shades of brown. A tower shaped like a thin pyramid seemed to lean over and peer down into the salon. Alicia peered upward at the crown of this pyramid and looked beyond into broken decking which thinned into darkness.

"This is one of five reciprocating engines that the Titanic used for propulsion. Some four and a half stories in height, it is as tall as Nautilus measures from keel to sail. This is the motive power that carved through the Atlantic and drove an iceberg deep within Titanic." Alicia gaped upward.

"It's hard to believe that all this old machinery worked as well as it did."

"Is it so hard to believe?" queried Nemo. Before she could respond, he added thoughtfully, "Yes, I suppose it would be for those who don't have an extensive background in things mechanical. It was purely chemical and mechanical processes without the control of electronics. The limits were set by the designer's facility or lack of facility in channeling physics. It's remarkable, really."

"Are we going to dive this area?" Alicia asked.

"You seem hesitant."

"Well, I understand your point of how large the engines were compared to our vessel, but this part of the wreck doesn't hold the same interest for me as it does for you or someone with your background."

"I see your point," Nemo responded, as though he was reading from a script, "but do you know the real powerhouse, the real source of Titanic's energy in her last moments, even as she slid beneath the waves?" Alicia did not respond, but only stared at Nemo. Momentarily, Nemo turned to his wrist interface and spoke into its receiver, "Conseil, bring us back so that the port side of the salon is just off the widest gap in the hull."

"Aye, sir. This will take a few moments."

"That's fine. Carry on."

A few minutes later Alicia could feel again the Nautilus settle onto its skids. Remotely controlled lights poured into the blackness and Alicia began to look about the wreckage of machinery that, even undamaged, would be unfamiliar to her. But then she saw them.

At first, there were some bits of cloth jutting out from the twisted pipes and piles of coal. It wasn't just cloth, though, it was clothing. Just as one realizes the image presented by a pointillist painting, Alicia traced the pattern and comprehended human forms. The clothes were bloated with the bodies still preserved by the mineral rich, freezing water. Alicia took in the scene again and then picked out a hand jutting from beneath a pile of broken steel—still reaching in the eternal moment toward a rail, now bent and beaten down. Suddenly, she recoiled at the image in her periphery.

A face, with expression yet of its final moments, hung beneath a gently waving mop of reddish blond hair. The attached body hung from a twist of piping and a partially collapsed platform. Alicia covered her face between her hands and turned away.

"Oh, my God! My God!"

Nemo stood aside and watched her with curiosity.

"Why? Why was this never recorded before?"

"A good question, Alicia," Nemo answered her at once. "Certainly, any of the remote vehicles used to film the various documentaries could have captured these grisly scenes."

"Why not, then?"

"Perhaps because it would certainly have ruined the commercial appeal, even for the jaded and calloused viewing public."

Alicia was about to respond but then caught herself. She remembered her earlier promise to herself not to spark conflict. Yet, as she considered the facts before her, she didn't completely disagree with Nemo.

"Would you like to capture this onto video as well as still photographs?"

Alicia looked up into Nemo's eyes and could tell he was not antagonistic but absolutely sincere. "Yes, I would, but it's so cluttered..."

"Oh, no. We can't dive this section," corrected Nemo, "Ulysses would have to do it. The dangers are far too great here. You can control Ulysses and the video as well as photography remotely from here," Nemo pointed to the painting that had served as the computer interface which had provided maps of the Southern Ocean before their passage into the caldera.

"Oh, right. Thank you."

"Of course," responded Nemo, with genuine appreciation for Alicia's journalistic interest.

36
Symptoms of Avarice

For over three hours, Alicia directed Ulysses' every move and supervised every minute of video and took nearly a thousand photographs, some in color and some in black and white. In addition, ultrasonic imaging revealed a tomb under the piles of debris pouring all around the base of the massive reciprocating engine. Alicia worked as the high-caliber journalist she was, with a strictly business demeanor. Once she was satisfied with the work, Alicia sought repast, "I could really go for one of those tuna sandwiches and chips again." Nemo arched his eyebrows in surprise at her hunger despite having been immersed in such morbid documentation for the past few hours.

"Yes, of course. Steward, you heard the lady. And I'll have a cup of coffee."

"Sir," the robot acknowledged the order and quickly stepped out of the salon.

"No snack?"

"No, I'm afraid that I don't have much of an appetite."

"Too bad. Nemo, this is fascinating!"

He only nodded his head in agreement. "If you'll excuse me, Alicia, I need to attend to a few things while you eat."

"Right. What about your coffee?"

"Hmm? Oh, you drink it."

Nemo left her in the salon looking out into the tomb of the engine room. He walked briskly toward his room. Once in, he locked the door and walked to the simple desk that held his diary and pens and threw himself into the lightly padded chair. "Damn it!" he spat. Nemo knew the signs. The initial shock had long since been dissolved and absorbed; there was nothing to check the avarice of the treasure hunter. "She records the tomb of a hundred men in the starkest setting of tragedy imaginable —and asks only for a tuna sandwich!" Nemo crossed his arms and stared at the floor in silence. Her greed would probably be her demise. It is what has driven her career, what drives her curiosity—not unlike his own. But this lack of respect for the past, for the dead, Nemo could not sympathize with it. This conclusion touched upon a recollection that caused him to shift his attention to another, yet related matter.

Nemo pulled open a drawer and took out an exquisite leather and wooden case. He opened it and looked down at the large luxury watch that looked back through a crystal held in place, oddly enough, by a rusted steel ring. "DNA of Famous Legends," Nemo pronounced the advertisement with scorn and a frown of disgust. The watch by Romain Jerome was constructed of actual steel from the Titanic. According to the marketing, it not only embodies great horology, but soul. "Damned grave robbers!" he huffed.

Nemo had used a system of aliases and cover addresses to purchase ten of the watches that cost more than twenty thousand dollars each. He tried to purchase more, but questions were being raised about the mysterious connoisseur who was trying to corner the market on these collectibles. It wasn't much, but it would have to do. These watches with their precious rusted steel from the grave would be returned to their resting place.

Nemo took the single watch and closed the lid of its case. He then opened another drawer and removed a similarly made but much larger box. Unfastening the latch, he opened the lid and placed the watch he had just been examining next to nine of its fellow copies. Each one was different in that the corroded steel bezels were all unique. With the latching of the box, Nemo again turned his thoughts to Alicia. He would have to keep a close eye on her. Nemo was not a superstitious man, but he knew his experience and did not let his reason obfuscate his observations, despite the absence of scientific explanations. Shipwrecks, though ruined, are very rarely dead; they don't often give over their contents without a struggle, especially those that went down with great loss of life. Even the galleon they had taken apart gave a last show of arms against the modern steel and laser weapons of excavation as it attempted to crush Ulysses under its own collapse. Alicia would probably try to pillage the wreck and he could only hope that Titanic would willingly relinquish a few more artifacts after so much had already been taken. If not, he was not going to risk his life to save hers. She could haunt that wreck with the others who still moved about the sad, barren decks.

37

THE BOARDING PARTY

Nemo was entering the salon just as Alicia was leaving it.

"Oh, where are you going?" Alicia asked, "The shielding just closed over the salon and I could feel that we were moving, so I assumed we were diving right now."

"Well, your suggestion of eating is a good one, and I'm going to need my energy as much as you will." Nemo walked toward the large table where the remains of Alicia's lunch still lay.

"A quick sandwich?" Alicia suggested.

"Heavens, no! If this may be my last meal, I want it to be a worthy one. I've ordered a grilled swordfish with scallops and pasta."

"Yes, but we'll be in position to dive soon," she reminded Nemo.

"Aren't we eager? Well, it'll be there and no one is on our heels down here, so don't worry about it."

Alicia looked at him and, frustrated, shrugged her shoulders. "Have a seat Alicia, relax." She sulkily pulled out a chair and plopped down onto it. Without looking at Nemo, she began to play with her watch.

"Well, as long as you're going to make me wait, can you tell me how it was you came to save me from our incident, as you called it. How did that all occur anyway?"

"Well, I was in the Persian Gulf looking for Al Qaeda operatives on the water and was in a particularly shallow area when the alarm rang out. I knew better than to be that obvious about things; even Conseil tried to warn me off, but no, I kept on it. Well, I surfaced quickly and cracked your keel and then I backed the Nautilus off a bit. I came out with Ulysses to see what sort of people had tracked me and there you were, pinned beneath a collapsed support. Ulysses cut the beam and when I turned you over I recognized you. We brought you aboard and the rest you know."

"No, the rest I don't know," Alicia interjected.

Just then, the steward entered carrying a covered tray and, stepping to the side of the table, began to serve.

"Would you like to join me?"

"Don't change the subject. Why did you save me?"

Nemo cut a large hunk off his fillet and popped it into his mouth, chewing deliberately, yet quickly. He swallowed, took a long draft of ice water, and echoed Alicia's question, "Why, indeed? I don't know, Alicia. You obviously weren't armed and your body, crumpled under the weight of that beam, seemed so pathetic. There was a pang of pity, I suppose. Then when I recognized you...well, I don't know. Knowing who you were, I'm sure I realized that taking you aboard would be problematic. Perhaps I wanted someone to see what I have been seeing. Perhaps I wanted to show off to someone who matters. I don't know, really. I think, though, that I just acted on a whim. In any case, here we are."

Alicia stared at him and tried to glean more. Looking into his eyes, though, she knew he was telling the truth as far as he understood it, as far as he could at that moment comprehend it himself. "Well, I'm glad you did," she smiled. He returned her smile and continued to eat. As Nemo finished his last bit of scallops and pasta, Alicia jumped up and strode toward the back of the salon, "Come on! I can't believe you made me wait so long!" Nemo laughed despite his earlier misgivings about Alicia's motives regarding the Titanic.

"Head to the cargo bay, not the dive boot."

Whether she heard him, he couldn't tell until he stepped through the hatch into the bay. Alicia stood before Ulysses and another member of the robotic crew. Ulysses towered over her, his infrared sensors gleaming through a thin red band of light just below the space between the dome of its head and where the body began. The other robot was smaller but no less impressive. It held a steel box that had only a framework. Inside were tubes of various lengths and diameters. Hearing Nemo behind her, Alicia turned and asked, "What's he for?" pointing at the other crew member.

"Well, we may need assistance. Those tubes are made of the same mimetic alloy as our suits, except that they don't just match the force being applied to the ends, but exceed it by ten percent. In other words, they are used for spreading collapsed decks and debris."

"Oh." The gravity of the situation began to settle in for Alicia.

"I'll help you into your suit. Now remember, don't overexert your muscles or the mechanical response will be far more than what you wanted. Let the electro-mechanical motors do the heavy lifting."

In silence she stepped into the back of the suit and pushed her arms into the openings of the sleeves and then stepped into the legs.

"Make sure your fingers are fitted into the gloves."

"Just a second," she responded, "okay, they're good."

"Such an elegant little dress, but I need to zip it," quipped Nemo.

"Very funny, wise guy."

The fit was very snug and Nemo put more force on the closure.

"Alicia, press farther into the suit so I can close the back."

After some fumbling and leaning Alicia grunted, "This is as good as it—" a constriction moving down her back stopped her breath for a moment.

"Are you all right?" Nemo asked. He moved around to the front where he could see her face through the Perspex helmet. "You okay?"

"Yeah, it's just a little tough to breathe."

"You'll be breathing easier in a minute. Slow breaths," Nemo reminded her, "I'm going to close the helmet. You're going to hear a sucking sound, but don't worry; you have plenty of air within the suit." Alicia nodded her head. She thought of what was awaiting them outside the bay door. The suit was unsettling enough. Her thought was interrupted by the sucking sound, and she was glad Nemo had warned her or she would be screaming to get out. Nemo appeared in front of her.

"I'm going to suit up and we'll proceed. You can talk to me just by speaking normally in your helmet. Remember, what I say goes. Right?"

Alicia nodded her head in genuine obedience to the commander of the Nautilus.

In what seemed only a few seconds later, Nemo stepped up to Alicia and gave her the thumbs up.

"We're set. The bay door will roll up slowly and the water will gradually fill. Before we leave the bay, Ulysses is going to run another diagnostic to make sure our suits are operating properly."

"Okay," Alicia answered quickly.

Red lights began to blink and reflect off the large bay door. Then, almost imperceptibly, the door began to lift and the icy cold atmosphere of the Atlantic's cellar began to swirl in under the threshold. Alicia could feel the pressure of the water against her boots, but not the awful cold that surely was there. The water rose rapidly to Alicia's waist and then slowed in its progress.

Minutes passed as the water made its way past her chest and was touching the bottom of her helmet. A few minutes later Nemo spoke.

"You and I are submerged. Ulysses is running a scan. Give it a minute."

Suddenly Alicia felt that she possessed all the patience in the world.

"Take your time. I want to come back alive."

Nemo smiled to himself. At least she possessed some humility before her own mortality. "We're good. We can flood the rest of the bay."

In a few moments the red light changed from red to amber.

"Alicia?" Nemo called. "Alicia?"

"Yes."

"Right now, the Nautilus is hovering parallel with the Titanic's boat deck near the remains of the pilot house. There's about a fifty foot drop beneath us. We're going to step out. Start kicking and your boots will unfold built-in flippers. We'll swim to where the pilot house had been. Okay?"

"Yes, I just, just need a moment."

"Of course," Nemo reassured her.

Alicia peered out at the rusted over white paint glowing in the spotlights of the Nautilus. Below her was a space of just fifty feet to the bottom of the world. Above her pressed the Atlantic Ocean and all it contained.

The floodlights of the Nautilus illuminated the rust-scarred side of the Titanic. How that white paint still shone brightly above the black steel plates! Even this broken forward section was at least as long as the Nautilus. So this was it, the ruins of the greatest maritime tragedy, an Atlantis unto itself. Other than Nemo, she stood where no one else had ever! She was ready to walk among those ruins now.

"Okay, I'm ready."

"All right. I'm going to go first. You follow me. Remember, when you kick, the flippers will emerge."

Nemo pushed up and off the flooring of the cargo bay and instantly his flippers popped out from the side of the soles of his boots. Easily, he began to cross over the space between the two great ships. Just fifty feet out he turned and tread, watching for Alicia.

"Nothing to it, Alicia. Trust the equipment; it'll work."

Alicia held her breath and pushed off as Nemo did. Frantically she began kicking vigorously. Not only did the flippers spring into action, but the sensors in her suit compensated for her exaggerated movement and signaled the motors to assist. After a moment's lag she shot upward as though she were holding onto a tow line from a boat.

"Too much, too much, Alicia! You swim like you drive. Slow it down and tread easy." Irritated at her own sense of panic, she complained about Nemo's engineering, "Well what kind of suit is this that doesn't work right!?!" Nemo said nothing and just repeated his command to tread easy. Slowly, Alicia descended to where Nemo was.

"Okay, I think you have the hang of it. We'll proceed to the bridge, or at least the remains of it."

In silence they swam on for half a minute, with Alicia in the lead.

"Alicia, slow down. You need to conserve your strength," Nemo reminded her, "the body is under unique stresses."

Without saying anything, she slackened her pace. Alicia knew that Nemo was correct and he knew that she was much too excited to be able to take it slowly. Just then, solid structures began to materialize just below them: glimpses of railing, then corners and angles of steel.

"Alicia, move up to that space that is curiously empty. That's where the binnacle and wheel used to be, before the tomb raiders stripped it."

"How do I land this thing?"

"Just straighten your back and position your legs as though you were going to sit. You'll set down on the deck."

They both stood where the tense crew had looked out into the darkness of April 14, 1912. Alicia tried to look out past the bow much in the same way the crew had tried. Despite the lighting from the Nautilus, she could make out nothing but the triangular shape of the ship's bow as it pushed out into the eternal night of the Atlantic. She concluded that this is probably all that the crew on watch saw as well. She imagined being in Captain Smith's shoes on that night. Would she have made the same decisions? It was all so easy in retrospect. She wondered at the sense of chivalry to save the women and children first. Yet still alive, the Victorian imperative to save the ideals of womanhood and home ran deep throughout the ship's travelers. She reflected upon the fact that in her own journalistic discourse she had often derided this sentiment. Yet now it was not artificial or pretentious. No, the heroism tested true. Her thoughts were interrupted by Nemo repeating her name.

"Alicia, Alicia? Shall we walk back toward the break of the front section?"

"Yes, this is surreal, though."

"It is, indeed. The size of the wreck and its silence are incongruous. But you'll see more."

Nemo and Alicia turned and made their way down from the bridge and with Nemo slightly ahead, began to walk the promenade that hadn't felt human footfall in almost a century. The iron depleted steel cracked under every step. Nemo commanded, "Ulysses, standby for emergency evacuation; keep pace with us, just parallel of the wreck."

"Aye, sir," came the baritone reply of the giant robot.

Alicia looked into the windows of the remaining superstructure. There wasn't much remaining from the millions of gallons of water that had rushed through during its two mile fall to the bottom. A few instruments remained affixed to the walls and some conduit, but that was all. Alicia kept her eyes averted from the starboard where the lights of the Nautilus were blinding her. The crunch of the decking under her feet combined with the brilliant spotlights began to wear on her nerves.

"Alicia, stop."

She froze in her spot. "We're at the end of the forward section that had broken off.

We're going to swim out a bit and then turn around facing the bow. There is a huge lighting rig behind us that will light up the severed decks. We'll then proceed down some of the corridors. Be sure not to look at the lights; it could cause some temporary damage to your eyesight. Once inside, we'll be using our own lights in conjunction with those of the rig. Is that clear?"

"Yes, all clear," she confirmed.

"Okay, just swim out as we did from the Nautilus."

Nemo stepped off first and Alicia closely followed. They kicked easily, and Nemo took her arm and led her to about the halfway point of the Titanic's ninety-two foot width. "Okay, Alicia, turn around and face the bow." She obeyed, and Nemo asked her if she was ready. She gave a thumbs up and Nemo ordered, "Ulysses, activate the lighting rig." Instantly the back of the Titanic was ablaze in white incandescent light. So powerful was the beam and volume of light that Nemo and Alicia did not cast shadows. Alicia's mouth opened in wonder as every deck was revealed down to the mud mantle that gathered around the lower levels. It looked like the back of a dilapidated apartment building.

The sight was just as impressive as her first look at Titanic, though the angle and features were vastly different. She could see into various compartments and it appeared as a giant discarded dollhouse, complete with furniture and the stuff of everyday life.

"Where would you like to begin?" Nemo broke upon her reverie.

"Well, I just don't know. You've done this before, so what do you suggest?"

"Most of the third class compartments are inaccessible as the lower portion of the ship took the brunt of the impact as it crashed into the bottom. Second and first class decks are more or less open."

"Okay, lead the way."

Nemo paddled just ahead of her and descended. Alicia followed Nemo a few deck levels from the very top and as they neared the jagged opening of a corridor, Nemo paused and slowly spun to face her.

"Alicia, once inside you'll want to say 'Nav lights, on' and your headlamps will come on. Don't scurry off someplace and not tell me. Whatever you do, don't lean against any walls or anything that even looks like a structural support, be it a column, railing, even the bulkheads are suspect."

"Yes, yes, of course!" Alicia retorted. She was excited as well as a little annoyed at Nemo's patrimony. Without responding, Nemo turned and began to slowly paddle forward. His headlamps lit the way and then Alicia's doubled his.

"This is a main corridor connecting some of the second class state rooms with a larger common area toward the end."

Alicia mechanically moved her legs as she looked about at the flooring that undulated in minor waves, the result of the enormous forces exerted throughout the ship from the collision into the sea floor. The walls were bare and the rooms were open, the doors having either rotted away or been torn off. Something caught her eye in one of the rooms. "I want to go into this room!" Nemo slowly turned onto his back and faced her. He was blinded by her headlamps.

"Say 'dim'."

"What!?!"

"Say 'dim'—you're blinding me!"

"Oh, sorry. Dim!" Instantly her headlamps cooled to a steady glow.

"Now, what do you see?"

"I want to see this room; there's something in it."

"Go ahead."

Aware of her bulky suit, Alicia slowly made her way through the doorway and then righted herself, allowing her feet to rest upon the bare flooring. A couple bunks were attached to one wall and a small bedstead sat with its headboard against the wall as though all was normal. A small bureau lay on its side, spilling some of its drawers in a careless pile. Instantly, Alicia moved toward the bureau and carefully grasped its top. Instantly, the water around her was filled with a fine sediment that blinded her. Instinctively, Alicia held her breath. She stopped and waited until the cloud began to dissipate. She then pushed and lifted the top of the bureau. The motorized dive suit compensated for the extra resistance, and the bureau came up easily and Alicia stood it upright.

More sediment rose and swirled in eddies around her, but she refused to stop her work. She began to open the drawers, looking for anything of interest. She went through a few drawers when something glinted in her lower periphery. On the floor in the pile of silt that had been disturbed, she spied a small golden loop. She bent down and scooped up the pile. Probing with two bulky, gloved fingers she pulled out a man's pocket watch. The gold shone and scintillated in the beam of her headlamp. She held the watch closer and stared hard at its face. The hands were still there and faintly the numbers could be read. She squinted at some letters in the center: "H-A-M-T-N... H-A-M-T-... is that an O?" she wondered aloud.

"Hamilton!" Nemo barked into her audio receiver.

Unnoticed, Nemo had settled in the doorway and had been watching her the whole time.

"It was an expensive watch for a second class passenger in 1912, especially in gold. The owner was probably moving up in his profession. It is just one of countless artifacts."

"It means so much then—to me." Alicia closed her fingers over it.

"Let's move on, shall we?" goaded Nemo.

Without a reply, Alicia moved to the door and eased her way through. With a sharp kick, her flippers reemerged and she was again gliding down the hall. Unseen, the bureau that she had worked over suddenly broke apart and collapsed, raising a silent, protesting cloud of debris.

38

As Passengers

Nemo moved forward without saying anything at first. His suspicions about Alicia's avarice were being verified. He thought about remarking further, but he knew that would only feed her sense of rebelliousness. He elected to move on and, he hoped, move past the incident.

"From here we can move upward and access the Turkish bath and swimming pool."

"Fantastic!" she enthusiastically replied.

Alicia looked around her, and as she swam, she ran her right hand along the wall. How many hands pushed against this very wall as passengers ran to the aft part of the ship, seeking the open air of that frigid Atlantic night? Something caught her eye as she was passing another stateroom. Without saying anything to Nemo, she paused, and pushing herself backward, she gripped the doorway with both hands and thrust her head into the room. Instantly, the room was alight from her headlamps. What looked like a cloak was lying very deliberately and almost theatrically on top of the remaining bed frame. Alicia eased herself into the room and let herself settle onto her feet. Momentarily, her flippers retracted and she made her way to the mysterious image. Again, the flooring creaked beneath her boots and one step brought a sharp crack that arrested her movement. But just for a second. Alicia watched as her gloved left hand, seemingly the hand of someone else, grasped the corner of the fabric. Instantly, it disintegrated, but before much of a cloud of silt arose, Alicia quickly turned the black mass over and found herself facing the partially skeletonized remains of a man. His eyes were gone, but his mustache waved to life in the disturbed atmosphere of his watery realm. Instinctively, Alicia pushed the ghoulish, grinning skull from her and with her shove, the entire body, cloak and all, flew into tiny pieces and sunk into the cloud of filth that was filling the room. Alicia turned and headed toward the doorway while she could still see. Scraping and more cracking shot out from beneath her footfall and as soon as she was clear of the doorway, she began to kick powerfully. In a split second her flippers snapped open and her legs, assisted by the motors in her suit, sped her down the corridor to where Nemo had been heading.

When Nemo heard no response to his comments, he knew without turning around to verify it that Alicia had seen the dead man on the bed. He also knew that the man's last position in death—perhaps he had had a heart attack and fell onto the bed—was no more. When she appeared at the end of the hall, Nemo acted as though he had not noticed she was late in following him.

"This large shaft at the end of the corridor would have been one of several grand staircases, and in this case, it opened into a first-class reception room. You can still see some magnificent stained glass, and some of the carved wood inlays are yet preserved."

Without a word, Alicia swam into the area and began to prowl the outside edges of the room. It was obvious that she was looking for something.

"What are you searching for, Alicia? You look like you lost your keys or something." "Oh, I don't know. I thought there might be something interesting, you know, an artifact."

"An artifact? What do you think you're in right now?"

"You know what I mean."

"Yes," Nemo paused in his reply, "I certainly do know what you mean," and there was an edge to his voice.

After she made her sweep of the room and determined that it offered nothing else but silt and broken light fixtures, Alicia asked, "Can we see the first-class state rooms?"

"I thought we'd see the Turkish bath."

"Is there anything worthwhile there?"

"The Turkish bath," came the curt reply.

"No, I'd really like to see the first-class section."

"Right. Swim up the shaft for the staircase. Much of the decking is gone as are many of the balconies. At the next deck level, the one just above us, go to your left. In other words, at the corridor's mouth, proceed aft. You'll find luxury suites, some of them well preserved."

"Aren't you going to lead the way?"

"No, you take the lead now."

Nemo could not see her face, but Alicia frowned and furrowed her brow at Nemo's sudden change in his approach. Ordinarily, she would not have trusted such a drastic shift in procedure, but she was too preoccupied by the prospects just above her. She briskly moved into the semi-circular opening and moved upward with a few brisk kicks. As she disappeared from his field of vision, Nemo pressed a small button on a console on his belt, a device Alicia did not have on her suit.

"Ulysses, stand by for potential extraction from Deck C."

"Aye, sir."

"Come down through the skylight and bring the crewman."

"Aye, sir."

Nemo released the button that cut out communication with Alicia and leisurely moved into the open space and then up toward the first-class accommodations.

Alicia had looked into a number of suites, but was disappointed to notice very few remains of any kind. A few picture frames hung on the walls, but their images were long since washed away. Farther down the hall, she came to a suite with a closed door. A closed door! This meant that none of the unmanned exploration vehicles that had scouted around the wreck had ever been in this part of the ship! Alicia gripped the door pull and attempted to move it down. She was met with resistance. She pushed harder and still, without movement, she strained further. The electric motors compensated and Alicia lost her footing as the frozen door handle pulled out of the door. The realization flashed across her face: she didn't need to gingerly open a locked door when she could simply break through it. She balled up her fist and brought it back to her hip in readiness for a strike, and with good form and rotation of the wrist to increase torque, Alicia shot the bolt of her arm. Her mailed fist easily punched through the semi-petrified panel of the door. That single blow weakened the rest of the door and it was an easy matter to simply pull the shards off the hinges.

Alicia couldn't believe how well preserved everything was. There were no human remains, thank goodness, just the accoutrements of posh furniture and finely wrought mementos. She let herself settle onto her feet and looked about as she waited for the flippers to retract. She noticed some wardrobes still intact. She walked toward one of them and noticed that the floor did not give to scraping and creaking as she moved. As she came to the large wooden closet, she noticed the fine carving of the doors and a magnificent cornice. She tugged on the door pull and the knob pulled loose from the water logged wood. "Still resistant, eh?" Alicia thought aloud. She stuck one finger of her alloy reinforced glove into the hole that had been left by the uprooted knob and, pausing a moment, gave a calculated sharp pull back. The door split widthwise and floated down to the uncluttered, relatively clean flooring.

Inside still hung neatly arranged dresses and frocks. The color was faded, of course, but nonetheless present in the glare of Alicia's headlamps. A coat hung at the far end and Alicia carefully reached into one of the pockets, and then into the other. Something was there, surely; she felt it even through the thickly padded finger tips of her gloves. She ripped the pocket downward and there it was—a brooch with a broken fastener at one end of a fine gold chain! The brooch depicted an ivory pelican feeding its chick with its own flesh. The detail was excellent as far as she could tell under the conditions of the light and increasingly silty water. Alicia reflected upon the irony of such artisanal skill and delicate detail spent to produce such a morbid image. She nonetheless placed it with the Hamilton pocket watch that she had deposited in a nylon pouch that was attached to her suit with a velcro patch.

Alicia looked about and noticed that some of the chairs were still upright and seemed sound. She walked over to the frame of a chaise longue and delicately lowered herself onto the middle portion of it. She looked about and imagined herself sitting back and reflecting upon her life as an Edwardian aristocrat. Yes, life was good if you were wealthy. As in slow motion, the chaise lounge began to fall back and downward. "Oops," Alicia muttered as she stood up while the furniture's legs broke down upon the floor. Unfazed, Alicia looked about her and noticed another closed door leading into another room, most likely a parlor of sorts.

She moved toward it, and as she came closer, she realized that it wasn't a closed door, but that something was blocking the doorway like the roof of a lean-to shelter. Whatever it was, it was tall and angled enough so that Alicia could squeeze herself under part of it while getting a good grip with her hands on the steel frame of the doorway. Turning her back to the obstructing object, Alicia backed up against it, and gripping with her hands, began to push with her arms. As she did so, she dug in with her boots and shoved back. She thought of working out at her gym and pushing the hundreds of pounds she would lift on the hip-sled. This time, though, as she strained, she could hear the normally silent electric motors whining. Whatever was obstructing the way wasn't wood or even the relatively thin steel used for the walls of the cabins. Alicia had no way of knowing this, but her suit was exerting nearly two thousand pounds of pressure per square inch. Suddenly, her breathing was labored and a cold sweat was breaking out on her face. She stopped straining as soon as she heard the crack, but then it was too late. She was numbly aware of falling backward and then nothing but blackness enveloped her. Her unconscious ears never heard the deep groaning of the stress that was shuddering through the ship.

39
RECONCILIATION

Nemo first detected trouble when Ulysses reported extraordinary strain on the electric motors of Alicia's suit and then the life support systems were being strained to maintain both temperature and electrical functions. Before Nemo could utter a word, the bellow of the collapsing steel filled his audio pickup; then a gust of water drove him backward toward the far wall of the staircase. Instantly, Ulysses jetted around and pulled Nemo to its chest while shielding him from the continuing current. With thrusters on full, Ulysses kept them both from being slammed into the opposite wall. After a few seconds, the pressure subsided and Nemo yelled Alicia's name into his helmet. There was no response.

"Ulysses, what's your status, damage report!"

"Negative on damage, Captain: all systems a-go," came the report.

"Scan for life; give me the situation."

The robot turned about and focused all sensors on the area as thunder still grumbled about them.

"Negative, sir."

"Negative what?"

"Negative reading from life support systems."

Just then Nemo's audio pick-up amplified the urgent voice of Conseil.

"Sir! Sir! Are you all right, over?"

"I'm fine Conseil, but our guest has had an accident. Can you pick up any readings of life from her suit? Ulysses is reporting negative."

"Just a moment, sir."

Several seconds passed and Nemo was growing impatient.

"Well, what of it?"

"One moment, sir. The signal is weak; there is heavy interference, the type caused by thick, very dense material."

Nemo checked his impatience. It would be a miracle if any signal could be had from among the mountains of steel and silt about them.

"Sir, yes. She is alive! The suit must be damaged in parts. I am getting a weak heart beat, shallow breathing, and...and that is all."

"Can you fix her location?"

"Yes, sir. She is in the boiler uptake casing just between Decks E and F."

"Decks E and F!?!" Nemo repeated, not believing what he just heard.

"Yes, sir," Conseil confirmed.

Alicia had fallen the equivalent of a three story building. There was very likely tons of debris that went down with her.

Nemo thought about his options. She had, through her greed, brought about this mess and now her life ebbed. Recovery would be hazardous to all involved and could cause complete collapse of the Titanic. If that happened, neither man nor machine would escape. Yet her life still stood in the balance between the present and eternity. Nemo thought of the hundreds of souls still haunting the decks of their doomed ship. What would they of the eternal night speak to him? What would they urge him to do?

"Conseil?"

"Sir."

"Extract her. Use all care and utilize the entire crew if necessary. Ulysses will be providing feedback in a few moments. Make haste. I'm afraid that broken bones are the least of her problems."

"Aye, sir."

Ulysses began to transmit data as soon as he was on the scene. Apparently, a section of the flue for some of the boilers had cracked and broken through the cabin wall that Alicia had been exploring. As she tried to push it out of the way, the shard of steel, weighing some twenty tons, was magnified by the considerable force exerted by her motorized suit. The rotted steel of the decking simply broke. She fell through and bounced once against the inside of the flue and then landed in a valley of angled steel and buckled decking that had punctured and blocked the flue as the Titanic had crashed into the floor of the Atlantic. Luckily, the biggest section of the flue missed her, but she was pinned from the waist down by chunks of decking and a shower of shorn rivets. As Ulysses used his cutting laser, Conseil sent a remotely operated, enclosed and pressurized emergency evacuation chamber to the scene. If Alicia's suit was in any way compromised, the crushing pressure of the ocean would kill her instantly. As she lay at the bottom of the giant ductwork, her suit was still functioning enough to keep her alive. Still, moving her might cause a failure in the alloy and consequently, her immediate death.

Nemo kept track of every stage of the operation and gave but few instructions.

"Conseil, send another crew member down with the evacuation chamber; Ulysses is going to need help moving the body without causing further damage."

"Aye, sir."

Nemo then addressed DOC. "DOC, full medic mode. Prepare the surgery for trauma and utilize any class two stewards for your needs."

"Aye, sir," came the steely reply.

"Conseil, I'll be aboard soon. Keep track of me and inform me when she is brought aboard. Get under way with medical treatment."

"Yes, sir!"

Nemo let himself drop to the bottom of the shaft that connected the various decks and what had been the grand staircases. Just at deck F his descent was stopped by a pile of mud and debris. He hovered just above it and took from a sack attached to his hip the case containing the ten Romain Jerome Titanic watches. Complete darkness crowded around him. He looked above and his headlamps shone upon broken decking and heavy-bearded rusticles. He felt the eyes of the dead upon him and he shuddered within his suit. "Forgive us our trespasses. Rest perturbed spirits, rest." Nemo somersaulted slowly and placed the box on top of the debris. Instantly, the silt arose and grasped the box with black, brown, and rusty fingers. It sank into the detritus and Nemo shook his head. After a moment, he kicked up with all that his tired legs could afford. The blessed motorized suit would take him back to the Nautilus with speed that he could never achieve on his own. Even with its help, he felt the fatigue of stress and physical exhaustion.

40
—
DUTY

Nemo lay upon the chaise lounge in the salon, occasionally puffing at a robusto. He reflected on the events of the day and came to some definite conclusions. For all her talk of justice and ethics — her condemnation of his actions, for instance — Alicia was without merit. It wasn't a simple matter of disagreement about a given decision or action; it was more basic and general in nature. Some things demand humility, respect. Her desecration of the grave, the hallowed place where all those souls perished on that great ship, belied her supposed high-mindedness. Despite his decision not to go out of his way to save her, he did do just that. Yet he felt no sympathy for her or twinge of sorrow. It was the right thing to do; it was consistent logic. One can't simultaneously honor the memory of the dead while allowing another's life to end.

What to do with Alicia was another matter. She was becoming unmanageable and potentially dangerous. Given her injuries, though, and the time needed for recuperation, she would be on board a bit longer. She wouldn't be fit enough to be dropped off at any port and to handle herself for a while. Perhaps she'd be content to undertake some study in the salon. Nemo smiled at his own suggestion. Journalists don't study; they report. Their remaining time together would pass, not as enjoyably as at first, but, who could say? Maybe having fallen into the abyss, she would have a new appreciation and respect for the watery world around her.

"Captain," Conseil's voice interrupted Nemo's thoughts.

Nemo swung his legs over the side of the cushion and sat upright, "Yes? What's the status?"

"The patient is in good condition. Her wounds will need constant attention, especially the laceration of the abdomen. No internal damage, but the wound was deep, requiring extensive stitching. She is currently receiving intravenous antibiotics and hydration."

"Is she conscious?"

"Yes, conscious and alert."

"Very good, Conseil. Download the complete medical program into one of the stewards and assign it to her care. I'm pulling DOC off her medical detail."

"Yes, sir."

Conseil swiftly turned to his assignment, and Nemo stood up and crushed out his cigar in a nearby shell ashtray. After a peremptory straightening of his tunic, he strode out of the salon and headed toward the sick bay.

.

41
STRAINED CONVERSATION

Nemo came into the room and paused as soon as he saw her face. She was looking much better than when he last saw the gray pallor and the blood stained, bluish, oxygen-deprived lips that were parted in a frozen gasp for air. She was merely pale now, and life was winning back the advantage every hour.

"Hello, Alicia."

There was no response, only a curling of the lower lip as though she were going to spit.

"What the fuck was that!?! Trust the equipment, my ass! I was nearly killed by your shit equipment!"

Nemo couldn't believe his ears. He was about to check this unexpected fire with his own talk of recklessness, stupidity, and greed, when he remembered that she had just been through a tremendous physical and emotional trauma, not to mention the possible side effects of anesthesia.

"You're obviously in no condition to talk. A steward will be placed in charge of your care and tend to your wounds and any of your other needs."

Nemo turned to leave when Alicia yelled back, "Where the hell do you think you're going!?!" Without looking back, he replied coolly, "You know where to find me."

Alicia's head swam in a sickening confusion of nausea, pain, and disorientation.

"Are you ill? Do you need to vomit?" asked the mechanical voice of the steward leaning over her. Alicia simply shook her head in the affirmative and a pan was propped under chin while the robot turned to a large wheeled cabinet and prepared a syringe. Alicia was gasping in an effort to keep the contents of her stomach in place while searing pain tore through her midriff.

"What...what's that?"

"This injection will settle your stomach. On a scale of one to ten, with ten being the worst, how do you rate your pain right now?"

"Ten!"

"I'll increase the pain medication as well. Try to relax; try to breathe easier."

The steward affixed the syringe to the port in Alicia's I.V. and depressed the plunger.

"You'll be better very soon." Alicia swallowed hard and pushed her head back into her pillow. Surprisingly for her, the pain and the nausea began to ease up in only a few minutes; her eyes grew heavy and she felt herself slide into the ease of unconsciousness.

As Alicia struggled to recover after her surgery, Nemo was finishing some modifications to the Cousteau. He stood within the cockpit and looked about the control panel to see if anything had been missed. Outside the window, Conseil could be seen packing several crates onto a flatbed truck. A large map case sat next to the co-pilot's seat. At first glance, the black leather blended in with the chair, but its size drew one's attention upon a second look. Nemo spoke into his wrist-link.

"Conseil, sweep again for any homing signals; do it now."

"Aye, sir. One moment."

Conseil bent his full attention to the electronic feedback that his sensors were tapping from both the Nautilus and the Cousteau.

"Negative, Captain."

"Very good. Clip the leads hanging from the open access near the keel and replace the panel with a welded plate."

"Aye, sir. And the equipment?"

"Inventory it with the other spare parts in the appropriate locker."

"Aye, Captain."

Nemo nodded and made his way down the stairs and into the salty atmosphere of the vehicle bay. Just as he was stepping from the bay into the corridor, his wrist –link sounded. "Yes?"

"Captain, the patient wishes to see you."

"How is her condition?"

"Good—she is sitting upright and is able to take fluids."

"I'll be there in thirty minutes," Nemo responded. "Conseil, have some fresh clothes brought to me in the Turkish bath."

"Very good, sir," replied the robot as it finished packing the last crate.

42
RECOVERY

Alicia received Nemo in a very different state of mind than when she had immediately after surgery.

"Please, Nemo, sit down. I want to talk to you."

Nemo did as he was requested and sat at the edge of the simple straight-back chair and looked into her face.

"I'm sorry for losing my temper earlier. I wasn't thinking straight and I know that I'm actually lucky to be here. You warned me about the structure being weak. Anyway, I just want to say thank you and I'm sorry for losing my temper."

Nemo stared into her eyes and then seemed to stare through her. Should he accept the apology? Should he accept it with a surly lecture on her reckless behavior that had certainly brought about the incident? Who was more reckless, though: Alicia, or Nemo who had brought her to the Titanic in the first place? It was like bringing someone who never climbed a foothill to the base of Everest and expecting complete success. Nemo sat back and crossed his arms, "It's all right, Alicia; it's all right. Everybody came back and, for the most part, in one piece."

"What happened? And what sort of injuries have I sustained? I have pain in the abdomen, but everything is wrapped up and the steward insists that I not remove the bandages."

"Of course. Yes, let me start with your injuries. A large sheet of steel had pinned you right about here," Nemo explained while drawing his hand above Alicia's abdomen. "You didn't have internal bleeding, but the muscles and skin were lacerated and required quite a number of stitches. DOC did his best to stitch in a manner that would leave minimal scarring. You'll need to take it easy for a while. I don't believe any wreck diving is in your immediate future."

"Don't worry about that," she smiled. "What happened, though? How did I end up this way?"

"Well, as you were trying to push your way through the blocked doorway in the stateroom, the combined force of the object you were pushing against, which was a sheet of steel that had broken off a collapsed boiler flue, and the considerable resistance of the mechanized suit, collapsed the floor. You ended up in the shaft that fed air into the boiler. A chunk weighing about seven tons came down on you. Its contact area was only about two inches, so it created quite a bit of force. The suits have a limit, of course, and you found it. To be honest, I'm not sure why the suit didn't decompress all at once given the damage. I'm glad it didn't, though."

"Yeah, me, too!" Alicia agreed. She wanted to leave discussion of that terrible experience behind and so changed the conversation.

"Nemo, were you able to save the things I found, you know—the artifacts?"

"Yes, whatever you grabbed was put into a preservation tank. You can figure out what you want me to do with them later on. We can treat them so they don't oxidize any further, or we can do partial restoration so they can be used on a daily basis."

Alicia smiled and her body seemed to relax and settle more deeply into the bed. Nemo left her to rest and made his way to the salon. It seemed that the next few weeks would be at least civil.

A few weeks passed and Alicia's recovery was going very well. She was engaged in some physical therapy to help restore some of the muscle damage she had incurred. A strict regimen of mineral baths had rendered her scar less pronounced than would have been possible in even the finest hospital. She was making progress, but still not ready for diving. Every day she charted the Nautilus' progress. Whenever she asked where they were going, he would only smile and say it was a surprise. Finally, the vessel stopped back in the Sea of Japan and settled in at a depth of about twenty-five hundred feet.

43
Krakens and Monsters

Nemo bounded into the salon carrying a collection of rolled maps and sheaves of paper bound by rubber bands.

"Well, we're here!"

"Where's here?" asked Alicia, turning her bright eyes on him.

Nemo paused before he responded. Her hair was up, with the Spanish comb holding the dark waves in place off her slender neck. Her blouse was a deep purple that complemented her complexion and showed off her fine form. She wore light, cream colored pants that were more closely fitting than Nemo remembered. She was lovely and he couldn't deny that to himself.

"We are in the prime area of squid traffic, and not just any squid, I'm taking about Architeuthis dux, the Giant Squid!"

Alicia's hands came together in a sharp clap, "I knew it! I thought we might as we approached the Sea of Japan, but I wasn't sure. I was hoping, though!"

Nemo beamed at her through light eyes and a wide grin.

"Do you think you're up to diving with them?"

Alicia's smile suddenly dropped. "I don't know, Nemo. I'm still pretty sore and my range of motion is limited. Also, I haven't mentioned this, but I get really tired after about midday."

Nemo listened intently, moving his head up and down as Alicia spoke.

"Of course, of course," Nemo sympathized, "I wouldn't dream of pushing you to risk reinjury. There's another possibility, though. I have what I call the Pilot. It's a small, single person sub that looks like one of those submersible scooters that are used at Caribbean resorts. The difference, though, is that the Pilot is completely enclosed, can dive to a thousand meters, and it uses the same propulsion technology as the Nautilus, except in miniature. The whole unit weighs only about nine hundred pounds."

Alicia's expression brightened at this possibility. "How close can I get with this thing; won't it spook the squid?"

"Well, you won't be able to get very close, but the Pilot has a magnified section of the viewing bubble that will enable you to get a closer look without getting so close as to scare off the squid. It's the best I can manage without you actually donning the dive suit. And as far as that is concerned, I agree that you ought not push yourself."

Still skeptical, Alicia turned her eyes downward toward the carpeting.

"I'll have it camouflaged," added Nemo, "the paint scheme will match exactly the hues and spectra at this depth. Give it a chance."

Alicia considered this and responded, "Well, you should have told me from the beginning that I was getting a camo-painted submarine—you're on!"

Nemo unrolled the various maps he had brought, some of which looked to be at least a century old.

"Where did you get these, and why are you using such old information?" Alicia asked. "Well, we tend to discount older sources because at the very least, they are suspected of inaccuracy and at the worst, they are seen as being embellished, especially with regard to creatures like the kraken. This premise isn't entirely invalid, but it tends to be taken at face value.

These older maps were acquired from whaling companies of the period. Accuracy was essential for profitability. Sperm whales fed upon the squid, of course. A larger concentration of whales could mean a larger concentration of their food source. A lot of squid was observed in the stomachs of sperm whales that were hunted for their valuable oil."

"I see," Alicia responded, "but don't you think that that feeding patterns have changed, especially with the overhunting of whales and the shifts in climate?"

"Salient point, Alicia," Nemo responded appreciatively. "Keep in mind that the protection of Sperm Whales has been effective. There are over a million estimated to be in the world's oceans. The feeding grounds and the ecosystems they include have been rehabilitated and because of their depths, they were the least disturbed and recovered relatively quickly." Where there's the cachalot, there is the kraken."

Alicia wrinkled her brow slightly in skepticism and Nemo saw that she knew he would not rely on the old maps alone.

"So you're going to just cruise on in there and look for the squid in your six hundred foot leviathan?"

Nemo smiled coyly. "Well, Alicia, I am using the maps as a start; they have nearly a century's worth of success to support their use. As for the finer details, I have developed a probe that is about half the size of Ulysses. It very quickly and quietly travels through the water with a passive sonar system and a special spectrum radar. The passive sonar takes in sound, especially the clicks of hunting whales. The radar uses pulses of ultraviolet light at a very high frequency. It does not disturb the marine life, but records the shadows they produce in the ultraviolet spectrum. There is about a two second interval between the flash and the recording of the image. It isn't quite real time, but close enough for our purposes, especially since the animals don't seem to notice it."

"As usual, there doesn't seem to be a problem you haven't planned for," Alicia concluded.

Nemo smiled rather smugly, but then paused, adding, "Keep in mind, Alicia, I have done this before, so this isn't uncharted territory for me."

"Well," Alicia brightened, "let's take a look at that little submarine."

Back in the hold that contained the Cousteau, Alicia sat in the cockpit of a craft that was more vertical than long and had a disproportionately large canopy. It resembled the larvae of some water insect.

"So how can I see anything? Isn't it going to be pitch black at this depth?"

"Yes, and that's partly why this canopy is so large. The acrylic looks like an ordinary formed piece like what you would see on a small plane or even the windshield of some recreational vehicle. It's actually a complex layering of different angles of photosensitive lenses sandwiched together. In essence, it is a large eye that draws in the surrounding light and focuses it to a point directly in front of you in an area that's about twelve inches square. That's why we don't need spotlights and that's why we aren't as likely to spook the squid as others have with their clumsy equipment."

Alicia raised her eyebrows in amazement. "Nemo, this is brilliant!" and she meant it. "Oh, I can't take the credit for this design, Alicia. The squid taught me. It is an imperfect replica of the squid's giant eye. That's also the reason why the Pilot needs camouflage. For some reason, the submersibles that are sent down from whatever research group are painted white or orange, as though an animal that lives its life in these depths and has an eye the size of a basketball won't see it. Morons!" Nemo shook his head and laughed sardonically.

"So don't you need a similar sub?"

"No, I've switched out the typical helmet in my dive suit with a canopy similar to this. The breathing device has been moved to the back, just below the shoulder blades."

"Well, then, Nemo, when do we go?"

"As soon as we get some signs of life."

Nemo set the probe out and it began sweeping a grid a kilometer before the Nautilus. Moving nearly silently and flashing its ultraviolet pulses, the data were transmitted back to the Nautilus. Nemo and Alicia both watched the screen in the salon while munching sandwiches. A sub screen opened within the larger readout and the clicks of hunting sperm whales came through the speaker.

"Ah, the real squid experts have arrived," Nemo announced, "give them about fifteen minutes and then we'll see where we're at."

"What's that?" Alicia asked, pointing to a purplish blob in one corner of an outlined grid.

"Ah-ha!" Nemo exclaimed clasping his hands. "That's one, a big one, too, hiding around some cover, a rock formation or such."

"Really?!?" Alicia exclaimed.

"Yes, the whales won't flush it out in such close quarters and it won't budge unless it absolutely has no choice."

"I thought squid were a match for the whales," Alicia wondered aloud.

"It's a battle to be sure," Nemo reflected, "but the whale's jaw is like a giant shear that not only cuts, but crushes the vital organs of the squid. Once the squid is between those jaws, it's pretty much over, despite the heroic efforts of the squid's arms and the formidable toothed suction cups."

"How do you match up with the squid?" Alicia challenged.

Nemo smiled and took a sip of coffee. "I've never had to resort to lethal force to preserve myself. Squid are aggressive but they are more curious. I've been very gingerly touched and I have also been violently grabbed and pulled toward that terrible beaked mouth. Before being bitten, the squid thrust me away, jetting off in the opposite direction. It knew from its sense of touch that I was inedible and essentially useless. It also understood that I was no threat to it."

"Weren't you afraid of being devoured or at least being maimed?" Alicia asked.

Nemo sat back and reflected upon the question for a moment. "You know, I really wasn't. And this isn't some show of machismo. I really wasn't afraid because it wasn't so terrible. It was just an animal doing what its species does. I was curious about its reaction, and I suppose I thought my suit gave enough protection, but you can never underestimate the power of an animal the size of the Cousteau. I was in its territory, in its world, and I sought it out. I had to respect its reaction."

Incredulous, Alicia stared at Nemo. She remembered the man who so coolly and dispassionately destroyed the crew of the boats laden with drugs. She thought about his precise, well planned sabotage of the submersible sent to recover the wreck of the yacht, the yacht he claimed as his own. She recalled their first meeting and his assurance to have her crushed and washed out of the bilge if she didn't comply with his orders. Suddenly she wasn't so secure in her assessment of Nemo's stability. Might he snap again and determine that this whole guided tour of the undersea world had come to an end?

Alicia watched Nemo as he stared at the screen. He was, for the moment, content to play the tour guide. He pointed to a readout that appeared within the larger screen. "Yes! The whales are gone, but he's still there. No time to waste—let's go!" Alicia broke off her dark reverie and was instantly as absorbed by the action as Nemo. She shoved back from the table and began to walk as briskly as she could manage toward the rear of the Nautilus. Meanwhile, Nemo barked orders into his wrist transmitter and followed closely behind her.

"Listen, I don't want to risk losing contact by taking the time to swim to the squid. I'm going to hitch a ride with you," Nemo hastily informed her.

"What about Ulysses?" Alicia asked.

"He's on stand-by for rescue. His presence is too powerful; the animals sense him and stay away."

It only took a few minutes, but it seemed much longer to reach the bay housing the smaller vessels. Nemo helped Alicia into her suit and then Ulysses did the same for Nemo. Alicia carefully climbed into the seat of the Pilot and noticed that the primary controls were identical to those in the Cousteau. Nemo's voice came through the speaker in her helmet.

"I'm going to hang on to this handle here on the side of the frame. Ease out of the bay and point the craft toward the large illuminated spot on the sonar field; that's the squid. Conseil will continue to upload its position relative to ours."

"How responsive is this thing?"

"It's a pretty gentle acceleration; throttle response has been calibrated to avoid lurching and quick starts."

"Okay, Nemo," Alicia said, giving him the thumbs-up.

Nemo gave the signal and the big light on the wall turned color as the door began to ease open to the streams of water first painting over the decking and then closing the gap to the ceiling. In a few minutes the two environments were one.

"Okay, Alicia, ease up and out."

Without a word she slid the controller while gently pushing the appropriate button for lift. The Pilot responded in a slow, yet deliberate way.

"Wow, I can't hear anything. Is the canopy so thick or is this so quiet?"

"A bit of both. Keep in mind how little water is displaced by this small vehicle."

"Nemo—it's moving!" Alicia interrupted him.

He looked through the canopy at the sonar and saw that the squid was moving out into the field before them. "Alicia, how close is it? What is the number in the lower right corner of the screen?"

"200," came the reply.

"Okay, that's 200 meters. Slow up and bring us to within about seventy-five meters and stop."

Far more quickly than if she had pushed the Pilot to its maximum speed, the squid had itself closed the distance. Alicia brought the craft to a stop and without a word, Nemo let go of the handhold and began to slowly swim toward the squid. Alicia broke her concentration on the sonar field and watched Nemo through the canopy. The periphery just forward of the Pilot was blurry, but the view straight ahead was clear and much lighter. Alicia gasped as she saw the mass of silvery flesh and billowing arms suspended in the water, like a kite resting between currents of the wind, fluttering, yet stationary. She saw Nemo swim in a horizontal plane within one length equivalent to the squid's body. He pulled up as though he were treading water and the two tentacles shot forward and grabbed Nemo by the torso and snapped him toward the mass of muscular arms opening to seize him. Alicia's mouth dropped open and she couldn't at first find her voice. "Nemo!" she screamed into her helmet. Instantly, Conseil's voice came in over her earpiece.

"The Captain has switched off his receiver so as not to disturb the squid, ma'am."

"Are you seeing this, Conseil!?!"

"No, ma'am. There is no video feedback."

"Oh my God! It's got him!"

"Ma'am, the Captain's suit shows no unusual stress levels."

Alicia couldn't believe what was happening. The squid was turning Nemo about, manipulating him effortlessly in its arms, testing his suit, gripping his limbs with increasing pressure. Suddenly, it shoved him away and is it did, Nemo tumbled in the dark velvet atmosphere of the ocean and finally righted himself in the position of a treading swimmer.

Suddenly, a bright, silvery shape shimmered past and the squid forgot about Nemo. Like the strike of a rattlesnake, the squid shot out its two tentacles and gripped the silver fish, but oddly, instead of pulling the fish into its mouth, the squid drew itself to the much smaller fish. Nemo looked on, confused at this incomprehensible reversal of physics. How does a larger body pull itself toward a smaller body? Then it became clear. The squid's tentacles had been secured to the silver fish — the silver fish was a lure tethered to a larger body. Nemo looked up as an oblong shadow began to descend even as the trapped squid was pulled upward. It was a submersible and it had angled the squid. Desperately, the animal struggled against the irresistible force of the line, straining its tentacles to the breaking point. Instantly, the ocean was filled with bright incandescent light. Nemo groaned at the sharp pain in his eyes caused by the magnification of his domed, canopy helmet. Even from a distance, Alicia shielded her own eyes from the brightness. The Pilot swerved sideways as a blurry mass pushed past the craft at a high speed. Alicia carefully looked up at the canopy, squinting. It was Ulysses that had sped past and was now near Nemo. Nemo climbed onto his back as Ulysses kept one of his arms extended toward the submersible.

The squid, certainly as blinded as they were, fought against the steel predator that had drawn it to its cold, inflexible side. The arms wrapped themselves around the sides and the protuberances of steel, but with no effect. Even Sperm whales flinch at the bite of the serrated suction cups against their skin. But this thing did not flinch, did not shake or move. Black ink clouded the water, but was dispelled by some current blowing from the monster's steel back.

Nemo looked on in rage. Undoubtedly, the men inside were videotaping the struggle. Every few seconds a tremendous burst of white hot light would magnify the scene, searing the eyes in a way that made the spine tingle. Nemo cussed and cursed within his silent helmet. He opened a compartment in Ulysses' back and began to dig within and throw out whatever came to hand that wasn't what he wanted. Pliers, a spare gill filter, a small axe, and bits of strapping all fell to the bottom of the world, until he found it. It was a small tripod, barely more than a foot in length.

Ulysses parted from Nemo and made his way to the submersible. He carefully skirted the craft, moving out of sight of the cameras; he positioned himself just over the fixtures that supported the lighting system that was the focus of so much commotion. The squid's struggle was nearly over. Exhausted and losing color quickly and with no more ink to try to dissuade its predator, the squid was dying. Ulysses had followed Nemo and kept within a few feet of his master. At a signal from Nemo, Ulysses moved above the submersible and unfolding a claw-like tool from the end of the right arm, he severed the main electrical connection to the underwater lights and cameras. The sea went black. Only the light from the tiny portholes could be seen glowing, unable to project into the dense night of the ocean.

The men inside spoke to each other in clipped sentences, checking and rechecking their gauges and readouts. Nemo stared at them through the submersible's ten inch thick acrylic porthole that kept out the terrific pressure of the water. One of the men noticed the scowling face outside the window and gave a start and yelled, pointing as his partner followed his gesture and did the same. The face outside the window was scowling, yelling, baring its teeth and occasionally pounding on the window. One of the men picked up a handset and began to speak into it. A final accusatory gesture, a pointing finger, was thrust at them.

Three small, black, round feet suddenly gripped the acrylic of the window. A small object, no more than the point of a pen, appeared in the middle of the three black points and paused. The men questioned each other and the one with the handset spoke into it, and then they stopped and turned toward that porthole. There was a noise so familiar, yet now so terrifying—the noise of a drill, a common electric drill. They began to adjust controls and instruments as the submersible attempted to rise to the surface as quickly as possible. The craft listed to port and the bow seemed unable to rise at the same rate as the stern. The dead squid, entangled in its tether, worked as a sea anchor and checked the submersible's progress.

Even without the squid's death grip, there was no time. In less than a minute, the carbide bit would bore its way into the acrylic far enough to compromise the structure. There would be nothing to help it. Only some fifty feet in their ascent, a tiny vein of water began to trace an almost imperceptible path from below the porthole's steel. The operator at his handset some quarter of a mile above at the surface could only hear the panting of the two men. And then he flung his handset down at the tabletop of the console where he sat.

The men most likely never felt the pain of being crushed to death by the steel walls that folded together. It was instantaneous, and a violent bubble of air was forced through the damaged porthole and made its way upward toward the surface. From a safe distance behind and below, Nemo looked on. The submersible, now nothing more than a crumpled ball of foil, dropped like a stone even as that cloud of air, still holding together its molecular grip, ascended. Nemo felt fatigue from the cathartic release. The lines of his face softened, and as he watched that mass of air pass beyond his sight, he wondered if it contained the souls of the two men.

He turned back toward the Nautilus and slowly kicked, but then stopped. Ulysses moved just ahead of him and then paused until Nemo was aboard his wide back. In a few moments, they were settling in the rear bay. The Pilot sat in its original spot.

44

ESCAPE

Nemo assumed that Alicia had asked to come aboard and that Conseil pumped out the bay, let her back in, and then reopened the bay for his and Ulysses' return. Tired and coping with a pounding headache, Nemo didn't ask about Alicia, but only asked the awaiting steward for some pain reliever and water. The robot simply obeyed, produced the requested items, and Nemo made his way to his room where he sprawled face forward onto his bed. He quickly fell into an uneasy slumber, his face lined with the sharp emotion of the nightmare.

Nemo awoke to the sound of a blaring horn. Disoriented, and drenched in sweat, Nemo sat up, cupped his ears against the noise and staggered into the corridor. Conseil and DOC suddenly flanked him. "Shut that damn thing off!" Conseil accessed the command module and the noise ceased. "What the hell is going on!?!"

"Sir, the bay doors have been opened and the Cousteau has been taken!"

"What!?!"

"The bay doors have been opened and the Cousteau has been taken."

Nemo quickly snapped out of the fog of exhaustion. "Any damage, any sign of sabotage?"

"Unknown, Captain."

"Full scan, I want every diagnostic run including ventilation and plumbing. Check everything."

"Aye, sir!"

"DOC, muster all hands and search every locker, galley cabinet, and space in the vessel for the passenger. Use infrared and carbon-dioxide sensors."

"Aye, Captain."

"Go to, gentleman!"

Each robot hurried off to do his master's bidding.

Nemo returned to his room and sat at his desk. A smile slowly crept across his face. Alicia never left the bay. She simply climbed aboard the Cousteau through the safety hatch that was always left open and from within the vessel opened the bay doors and sped off. He nodded his head. The destruction of the submersible was the last straw for her. The motivation of fear or anger was too powerful, and the opportunity presented itself.

Searching a six hundred foot vessel for a single person would be time consuming except for a search party as well equipped as DOC, Conseil, and the robotic crew. In less than half an hour, both appeared outside of Nemo's room. Conseil spoke first, "Sir?"

"Yes, Conseil?"

"Everything appears to be in order."

"Very good. DOC, what have you found?"

"Negative, Captain, all secure."

"Good."

"Captain?"

"Yes?"

"I'm tracking all contacts and there are three vessels directly overhead. At the appearance of the submersible, there had been two such vessels. The chances of the third being the Cousteau are..."

"Oh, Conseil, I'm sure you're right," Nemo interrupted.

"Battle stations, Captain?" DOC offered.

"No. Our passenger has made a choice and we're going to respect that choice. No retaliation, no recovery of the Cousteau. Undoubtedly, she is telling them about us, our capabilities and, as well as she can reckon, our strategies. An urgent call has by now been issued and any and all U.S. and allied naval assets are setting a net around a two-hundred mile radius."

"Captain," Conseil rapidly replied, "with our superior speed, we could be outside of that radius before that perimeter has been established."

"Perhaps, Conseil, but I would prefer to let our enemies think that we have slipped their net without actually having done so."

"Captain?"

Nemo paused for a moment before responding. "Conseil, as I recall, there are a number of deep water caves and subterranean tunnels hereabout."

"Very good, sir!" Conseil responded, his tone expressing unmistakable pride in his captain.

"Find the closest, deepest, and most protected of these."

"Aye, sir!" Conseil saluted with alacrity and turned to his task.

"DOC, we're going to operate in stealth mode. Lower the sail; seal all bulkheads. There is a good chance that a more capable sonar net will be set this time. Silence is critical. Everything must be secured and all nonessential mechanical components are to be switched off and muffled. I mean everything, including the grandfather and mantle clocks. Switch off all nonessential electronics and disconnect non-hardened equipment."

Aye, sir," came the usual reply and the robot set off to complete his tasks.

Nemo walked down the corridor to what had been Alicia's room. He entered without pause and slowly turned, taking everything in. The painting of the water-nymph held his attention and he thought of her outrage at the destruction of those men whom she considered to be innocent. Was she right? In her own mind, there was no doubt. In Nemo's world, a different set of principles applied.

He noticed her dressing table. The comb from the galleon was resting next to a hair brush. Nemo opened the drawer and noticed the preserved watch and the brooch from the Titanic. Her brother's Omega, however, was gone. Did she plan to leave when she did? Probably not. She was never without her brother's watch. If she had planned to leave, the souvenirs from the Titanic would certainly have been taken. The comb had come from Nemo and as such, would be tainted and therefore left behind. Nemo opened the wardrobe and looked absently at the clothes hanging there, waiting to be worn. He closed the doors and quickly turned on his heel and strode out. Conseil was approaching Nemo from down the corridor when Nemo spoke.

"Conseil, secure everything in the passenger's room and seal it."

"Of course, sir."

"So, what do you have for me?"

"If you would care to go to the salon, I can show you several options and one most interesting with regard to a subterranean passage."

"Excellent, Conseil!"

"Thank you, Captain."

45
RETURNING HOME

After two months in the custody of the U.S. Navy, Alicia was released under strict restrictions of what she could say about her experience. Of special interest to them had been the map case found in the Cousteau. It had been full of diamonds as well as a list of various coordinates for obscure ports and safe harbors in neutral countries. She insisted that somehow Nemo anticipated her escape and planted these items as damning evidence. Finally, and begrudgingly, the Navy satisfied itself that she was in no way colluding with Nemo and that she had to play a delicate psychological game to keep from stirring his homicidal wrath. Alicia told the Navy's technical experts everything she could manage about the Nautilus, the Pilot, Ulysses, DOC, even the refilling canter on the nightstand. It was not her fault that they laughed in her face when she told them of the dry dock underneath Antarctica.

Eventually, though, the Pentagon decided that Alicia Petit-Smith was the best piece of detection equipment they could ever have, and so they gave her the permission to publish a "tell-all" book and run with the talk show circuit until no one wanted to hear about it anymore. The glare of the media would be turned toward the waters, and Nemo would become less comfortable in his wanderings. Eventually, someone would find him and when he was found, they would be ready. All sub-hunting vessels were armed with the deadly Barracuda torpedo, the equivalent of a sniper's round for killing submarines.

For months, the Navy explored the area where Alicia surfaced the Cousteau. Based upon her recollection and estimates, they traced the courses most likely traveled by the Nautilus. The trail went cold, however. No other vessels were sunk and no sightings of the Nautilus were reported. The Navy called off the search, though a state of preparedness was maintained.

46
FAREWELL

Alicia's book, Into the Abyss: My Story of Survival, stayed on the New York Times Bestseller's List for months. Naturally, talk began of a blockbuster movie and major studios were competing, offering magnificent sums for the rights to her story. Alicia was quickly becoming a very wealthy woman. Beyond affluence, she enjoyed unparalleled influence. She enjoyed entrée to society and even governmental agencies at a level that she could have never imagined. In the course of her fame, she had convinced herself and continued to convince those in her vast audience that Nemo's time was now very limited and that she had singlehandedly done more to bring about his demise than the U.S. and allied navies.

Even the most hurried celebrity needs a place to call home. Alicia took up residence in a newly constructed, elite, high-rise condominium in Washington D.C. Nearly every cable talk and news show featured her. She was a guest on every show from Anderson Cooper to Jon Stewart. Entertainment Tonight even unleashed some paparazzi to keep watch on Alicia's private life. She had no shortage of eligible male celebrities sending her gifts and pestering her newly acquired staff with requests for dates.

So it was no surprise when Alicia answered a call from the front desk of her residence and was told that a number of parcels for her had been delivered. She asked that they be brought up and in what seemed to be just minutes since hanging up the phone, the packages were being placed within her foyer. Alicia poured herself a glass of champagne and lit a cigarette, her usual practice when opening the almost daily collection of presents. There were the usual trinkets of corporate hospitality looking for celebrity sponsorship, several proposals of marriage, and even the keys to the house of a newly minted Hollywood A-lister who was at least ten years her junior. It was typical since her "return from captivity", as she often described it. One unopened, rather plain brown box caught her attention, though, and she took a drag of her cigarette and set it down in the crystal ashtray she always carried from room to room whenever she smoked.

The plain, cheap label had no return address and simply read: Happy Anniversary.

At first she did not realize the significance of the message. After all, so much had transpired and so many people had chosen to commemorate what they thought were meaningful connections with her. As she pulled apart the top flap of the outer box, she looked inside and suddenly stopped what she was doing. There was that numbing tingle one feels when adrenalin courses too quickly and too hotly through the body. It was there as it had been months before: the black lacquered wooden box with the hinged lid. Carefully, as though she were handling an explosive, Alicia lifted the box from the brown carton and set it on the table before her. It was only within arm's length, but she peered at it as though it were across the street. Then, in one movement, she reached out and flipped back the lid.

Staring up at her was the Hamilton pocket watch and the brooch she had taken from the Titanic; a slip of paper was tucked within the lid. The note was written in Nemo's quick, slanted hand:

Remember, a man cannot lose either the past or the future: for what a man has not, how can anyone take this from him? ~N

Alicia slowly pronounced the name of the source of the quotation, "Marcus Aurelius." As she did, she slowly shook her head in affirmation of the message and its sender. She let her eye rest upon the single initial of his name and noticed how the curved lines resembled two undulating waves.

Made in the USA
Charleston, SC
16 October 2013

Finally, on November 13, 1956, the boy-cotters won a great victory. The Supreme Court agreed with three judges who had ruled that the Montgomery bus-segregation law was not legal. The ruling became official on December 20. It stated that black people must be allowed to sit anywhere they chose— front or back. Thirteen months after it began, the boycott was finally over.

Black citizens of Montgomery were relieved. They were glad that the law was finally on their side. They were glad the boy-cott had worked. But there was no big cele-bration.

"I don't recall that I felt anything great about it," said Mrs. Parks many years later. "It didn't feel like a victory, really," she said.

Many people remembered the bitter events of the past year. They had fought a long, hard battle, and now it was over. Perhaps they were sad that they had to fight it at all. Perhaps they knew that many more battles remained to be fought. The boycott

had been the first big blow to segregation. But many more such blows were needed before segregation would be defeated. It was a good beginning, but it was just a beginning.

Early on December 21, Dr. King, Mr. and Mrs. Abernathy, E. D. Nixon, and a white man, Glenn Smiley, got on a city bus.

As Dr. King paid his fare, the driver smiled. "I believe you are Reverend King, aren't you?" he asked.

"Yes, I am," Dr. King replied, smiling back.

"We are glad to have you this morning," said the driver.

"Thank you," said Dr. King, and he took a seat in the front of the bus.

Afterword

This story told how black people in the community of Montgomery, Alabama worked together to solve a problem. Some of the people in the community later wrote books about what happened. Those books were used in writing this story. Reporters wrote news stories about what happened. Their news stories were also used in writing this story.

Notes

Page 5 Laws that enforced segregation in the South were called Jim Crow laws. No one is sure where the name *Jim Crow* came from. But beginning in the 1890s, *Jim Crow* came to stand for any law or act that kept black people from doing the same things or going to the same places as whites. Black people had to sit in separate sections of movie theaters, parks, trains, waiting rooms, and restaurants, as well as buses. They could not use the same public restrooms or even drink from the same water fountains as whites.

Page 11 In Montgomery in 1955, there were 50,000 black people and 75,000 whites. About 40,000 black people rode the buses. Only 12,000 whites rode the buses.

Page 12 The idea of black riders boycotting the buses was not new. As early as 1900, blacks in 27 cities had boycotted streetcar lines. Blacks in Baton Rouge, Louisiana, had boycotted city buses twice in 1953. After the second boycott, only two seats in the front of each bus were "for whites only." One row of seats in the back was "for blacks only." Black and white people could sit in the other seats on a first-come, first-served basis.

Page 16 Mr. Nixon had been the president of the Montgomery NAACP (National Association for the Advancement of Colored People) from 1947 to 1951. He was president of the Alabama NAACP until 1952. He, too, like Mrs. Robinson, helped many black people register to vote.

Page 28 Mrs. Robinson was already a member of Dr. King's church, Dexter Avenue Baptist Church. She was on the Political Action Committee, helping people register to vote. She also worked for the NAACP.

Pages 33–37 The aim of the boycott was to show the power of the black community. Dr. King said, "We were withdrawing our cooperation from an evil system rather than merely withdrawing our economic support from the bus company." The bus company lost more than $750,000 during the boycott.

Page 37 Mrs. Robinson was an active member of several MIA committees. She became the editor of the MIA newsletter and drove her car in the car pool, mornings and afternoons, after teaching at the college. Dr. King said she was more active "on every level of the protest" than any other person.

Pages 37–38 A group of people from the MIA met with the mayor and a lawyer for the bus company. Not much came of this meeting. The lawyer was opposed to the changes the MIA members wanted. "If we granted the Negroes these demands," the lawyer said, "they would go about boasting of a victory they had won over the white people; and this we will not stand for."

Page 42 Members of the MIA had a second meeting with the mayor and white citizens on December 17, 1955. At this meeting, the mayor formed a committee of eight white people and five black people. The mayor wanted this committee to come up with a way to solve the boycott crisis. Mrs. Robinson was quick to point out to the mayor that the committee should have the same number of blacks as whites. The mayor reluctantly agreed.

Pages 42–44 The black ministers gave people lessons in nonviolence. They would line up chairs like those on a bus. They would ask a few people to sit in the chairs. Then they would have some other people play white passengers and bus drivers. The "white" players would taunt or provoke the black passengers. The ministers helped the people learn how not to show their anger and remain peaceful.

Page 45 The Montgomery bus company was actually owned by National City Lines, Inc., a company in Chicago. That company owned buses in 35 cities throughout the United States. After the Supreme Court ruling, the company made an announcement. It told its Montgomery drivers it was not going to disobey the court's orders. It said any driver who didn't want to obey the orders should quit. Six out of one hundred drivers did.

Richard Kelso lives and works in New York City where he is a staff writer for Curriculum Concepts. Mr. Kelso has also written *Days of Courage* and *Building a Dream* for the *Stories of America*.